AN INNOCENT IN HIS BED
A virgin—for the taking!

He's a man who takes whatever he pleases—
even if it means bedding an inexperienced
young woman....

With his intense good looks, commanding
presence and unquestionable power, he'll
carefully charm her and entice her into his
bed, where he'll teach her the ways of love—
by giving her the most amazingly sensual
night of her life!

Don't miss any of the exciting stories:

The Cattle Baron's Virgin Wife
Lindsay Armstrong

The Greek Tycoon's Innocent Mistress
Kathryn Ross

Pregnant by the Italian Count
Christina Hollis

Angelo's Captive Virgin
India Grey

Only from Harlequin Presents EXTRA!

D0982216

LINDSAY ARMSTRONG

I was born in South Africa but I'm an Australian citizen now, with a New Zealand-born husband. We had an epic introduction to Australia. We landed in Perth then drove around the "top end" with four kids under the age of eight. There were some marvelous times and wonderful sights, and ever since, we've been fascinated by wild Australia. We've done quite a bit of exploring of the coastline by boat, including one amazing trip to the Kimberley.

We've also farmed and trained racehorses, and after our fifth child was born, I started to write. It was something I'd always wanted to do but never seemed to know how to start. Then one day I sat down at the kitchen table with an abandoned exercise book, suddenly convinced the time had come to stop dreaming about it and start doing it. That book never got published, but it certainly opened the floodgates!

THE CATTLE BARON'S VIRGIN WIFE

LINDSAY ARMSTRONG

~ AN INNOCENT IN HIS BED ~

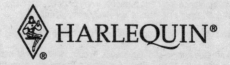

TORONTO • NEW YORK • LONDON
AMSTERDAM • PARIS • SYDNEY • HAMBURG
STOCKHOLM • ATHENS • TOKYO • MILAN • MADRID
PRAGUE • WARSAW • BUDAPEST • AUCKLAND

ISBN-13: 978-0-373-82367-3
ISBN-10:   0-373-82367-3

THE CATTLE BARON'S VIRGIN WIFE

First North American Publication 2008.

www.eHarlequin.com

Printed in U.S.A.

THE CATTLE BARON'S
VIRGIN WIFE

CHAPTER ONE

SIENNA TORRANCE packed her bag and prepared to farewell her patient for another day but Finn McLeod had other ideas.

He watched her out of dark blue moody eyes.

They both wore skin-tight stretch track suits and they were both drenched in sweat. But whereas she bent to zip her bag and straightened to wring out her honey-coloured pony-tail with lithe movements that showed off a compact, leggy figure with delicious hips, he was confined to his wheel chair.

That wasn't entirely true. On his better days, since a car accident had seriously injured his left leg, he could get about with a walking stick. But Sienna, his physio-therapist, always insisted he use the chair after a session with him. She even made a practice of ceremonially wheeling him out of his private gym back to the house and handing him over to Dave, his nurse, although the chair was motorized.

Not, for that matter, that he needed a nurse now, but Dave was also a trained masseur and he doubled as his valet and driver.

'Come in and have a drink,' he said abruptly as she started to push him.

'Oh, no, thanks, Finn, I do need to be off,' she replied—she had a fascinating, rather husky voice.

'Where to? Another patient? It's nearly six o'clock. A boyfriend?'

Sienna hesitated. 'No, but it's been a long day.'

'Or do you have something against fraternizing with me?'

Sienna grimaced as she manoeuvred the chair down a ramp and outside to a path that ran between thick, rich green lawns and riotously colourful flower beds. There were bees humming, birds calling and butterflies hovering.

It would be hard to find a lovelier property than hill-top Eastwood, she thought as they approached the main house. It followed the Queensland tradition of wide, covered verandas, steep roofs and double outside doors to capture the breeze, but rather than being wooden it was built of honey-coloured sandstone with a sage-green roof. It also had marvellous views down to the Brisbane River.

'I don't fraternize with patients,' she said carefully. 'Nothing personal!' she added on an upward beat. 'I'm also a working girl with a million things to do.'

'If you don't come in for a drink and a chat,' he said ominously, 'I'll put this chair on auto and drive myself into the river.'

Sienna stopped pushing and slammed a brake on. 'Finn,' she said quietly, however, after taking a deep breath, 'don't be silly. Look, I know how frustrating this must be. But you've done so well, I'm full of admiration for you! And the end is in sight now.'

It was true, she did admire Finn McLeod for his pain-filled perseverance towards regaining his mobility after the tragic accident that had claimed the life of his fiancée.

She'd rarely seen such will-power, and she had seen him often with his knuckles white and his teeth almost driven through his bottom lip as he'd doggedly pursued his rehabilitation.

She'd also acknowledged that through all this, he was still dynamically attractive even when he could be cutting and moody. Not that, for professional reasons, she'd ever allowed herself to dwell on it. Anyway, she regarded herself as fireproof when it came to men.

'Silly?' he reflected. 'I've got a business proposition to put to you, Ms Torrance, so I don't see anything silly about it at all.'

Sienna stared down at the top of his head. His thick dark hair was tousled and damp. She frowned. 'What kind of a business proposition could there possibly be between us?'

'You're going to have to wheel me on to find out.'

Sienna clicked her tongue in annoyance. She was used to humouring men, she often turned down outrageous propositions with a kind but funny retort, but it was the last thing she'd expected from Finn McLeod. What else could it be, though?

'Tell me now, Finn, then I'll be the judge of whether I have a drink with you or not,' she said coolly.

She saw his shoulders lift as if he was laughing inwardly.

Some minutes later, she was sitting on the veranda with a soft drink in a tall glass in front of her and he had his longed-for beer. There was a silver dish of olives and nuts on the table between them.

The drinks had been served by a middle-aged man he'd introduced as Walt the butler. They were now alone.

'Let me get this straight,' Sienna said. 'You want me to come out west with you so we can continue your treatment on a—on a cattle station?' She blinked several times, she had grey eyes and naturally dark lashes.

'Yep.' Finn McLeod sipped his beer.

'But why do you need to bury yourself—' she broke off and bit her lip because he hadn't that long ago buried his fiancée, '—uh—need to be on a cattle station out west anyway?'

He eyed her, then looked around. 'I'm going crazy up here. I need a change of scene. I was born out there and I like it.'

'Has it occurred to you that I only spend a couple of hours a day with you? That I might go insane on a cattle station for weeks on end? Or, that you most probably don't have any of the equipment needed? Not only that but you'll be away from your doctor.'

He shrugged. 'I've got his go-ahead and I can fly him out if necessary. Ditto all the equipment—there's already a gym and there's a pool.'

Sienna sank back and took the first sip of her soft drink; it was delicious, a blend of mango and orange with a dash of mint. Her thoughts were slightly bitter, however.

The McLeod family, now headed by Finn, was extremely wealthy and had diversified from cattle into many areas. She'd never doubted that, it was well known, as were some other facts about the dynasty.

Finn's parents had divorced and his father had remarried. The new Mrs McLeod, Laura, had presented Finn's father, Michael, with another son, eight years Finn's junior. The first Mrs McLeod had, according to popular belief, never recovered from the divorce and pined away. Some years later Michael and Laura had been killed in a plane crash. The pilot had been Michael's brother, Finn's uncle Bradley, who had perished too.

Alice, Finn and Declan's aunt on their father's side, had brought the boys up.

So it was a colourful dynasty with a tragic background, now added to after that terrible car crash when a drunken driver had ploughed into them and his fiancée had been thrown clear but killed instantly and Finn had been trapped in the car. But that didn't alter the fact Sienna found herself somewhat annoyed that Finn McLeod could virtually wave a magic wand to achieve his goals and, on top of that, expect everyone to jump to his tune.

'I'm sorry—' she started to say, but he intervened.

'As for your spare time, I happen to know that the Augathella Hospital would be more than happy to have the extra services of a fully-trained physiotherapist to call on for a few weeks.'

She stared at him incredulously. 'How do you know that?'

He raised an ironic eyebrow. 'I checked it out with them. The hospital is not that far, as the crow flies, from Waterford.'

Waterford was the principal cattle station in the McLeod crown.

Sienna licked her lips. 'I do work, you know. I'm employed by a consultancy so, apart from anything else, they would not be too happy for me to disappear beyond the black stump for several weeks. I do have other patients.'

'Your boss is quite happy for you to do it.'

Sienna put her glass down with something of a rap. 'Now look here, Finn, that's going too far! How dare you do all this behind my back?'

He shrugged. 'Just thought I'd clear the decks of any unnecessary objections you might be likely to make.'

'Well, that may be how you do business but—'

'It is,' he drawled. 'You'd be amazed how successful it usually is. Look—' he sat forward '—it's actually a feather in your cap. When I discussed it with your senior partner, he told me that you were establishing a growing reputation in accident rehabilitation therapy. I told him I could believe it, you certainly seemed to be working wonders for me and that's why I want you and no one else.'

Sienna blinked, then frowned. 'A feather in my cap? I would call it something else. A subtle way of twisting my arm and, I'm sorry, but I'm not going to do it.'

'Why?'

She regarded him for several moments. His glossy dark hair was still tousled, there were blue shadows on his jaw, he had a decisive mouth and a tapering chin. It was a memorable face—she thought suddenly that she'd probably remember it for a long time—and it was accompanied by a memorable physique. Finn McLeod was six feet four, broad-shouldered, narrow-hipped, long-legged and what had undoubtedly helped him along his path to rehabilitation was the fact that he'd been in prime physical shape when the accident had happened.

Why not? she thought. Yes, he was the kind of man many women would wonder about, but she didn't have that problem, did she? So was she worried about *his* motivation? Because she'd been well taught to be on guard against patient attachment where you became the focus of their lives?

But, from his point of view, was this the same thing or simply the machinations of a wealthy man entirely too used to getting his own way? Much more likely, she suspected.

'Finn,' she said slowly and choosing her words with care, 'any good physiotherapist could have done what I've done. Actually, *you've* done it. It's been your willpower. You don't need me, *per se*.'

'Afraid I'm falling in love with you?' he queried.

Sienna took an unexpected breath, then narrowed her eyes. 'Are you?'

'No.' He put his glass down and stretched. 'When you've had the best—no insult intended, Sienna—and lost it, you probably don't ever expect it to happen again.'

Sienna stared at him, frowning again. She couldn't take issue with the "best" tag because Holly Pearson, his fiancée, had been, in a word, glorious—and not only to look at. She'd taken the country by storm as a TV weather presenter, then become a TV personality in her own right, frequently appearing on talk shows and capturing audiences with her zany humour and her warmth.

But had Sienna detected a tinge of something she didn't understand in Finn McLeod's voice, something at variance with his words like the prick of a pin you hadn't known was there? Or had it been the bitterness he still felt about losing Holly? Of course, that had to be it, she thought and felt a rush of compassion for him.

'Are you?'

Sienna came out of her thoughts and looked at him. 'Am I what?'

'Falling in love with me?'

Her eyes widened and her lips parted. 'Have I ever given you the slightest reason to think that, Finn McLeod?' she retorted.

'On the contrary.' He grimaced. 'Although that doesn't precisely answer the question but, anyway, what is the problem?'

Sienna shot him a dark look. 'I don't like being manipulated. I resent the fact that you imagine I can just drop everything at a moment's notice—'

'A week.'

She waved a hand dismissively. 'I—'

'Look, think it over, Sienna. You can let me know tomorrow.'

She opened her mouth, then shrugged, finished her drink and got up to go. 'All right, but I don't imagine I'll change my mind. You should shower and change now. I'll call Dave.'

'Yes, ma'am,' he said meekly enough, but his dark blue eyes were full of satirical amusement.

Sienna swished her pony-tail and walked away.

She shopped for fresh fruit and vegetables on the way home.

Her apartment was small but pleasant, a second-floor flat in a two-storey building in the suburb of Red Hill, perched on the northern rim of the city.

It had cool tiled floors, white walls and all mod cons, but the broad balcony was her favourite spot. It was fitted with sliding insect screens, and had grand views of the city below. She had a table and chairs on it and a bevy of flowering pot-plants as well as an array of herbs—she loved growing things.

For the rest of her flat, she'd kept her decorating fairly minimalist to suit the climate. There was a sumptuous corn gold settee and two plain cane chairs in the lounge with moulded Perspex side tables. On one of the white walls she'd hung a large, lovely print of a girl walking on a beach at sunrise beside a calm, shining sea that seemed to draw you into its cool, tinted waters.

A beaten silver urn found in a market in Malaysia stood on her teak television cabinet and on the wall in her small hall a wonderful painting of three elephants, drawn as children might but delicately coloured and captivating all the same, greeted visitors. She'd found it in Thailand.

She'd found her garnet and sapphire rug on the lounge floor in Turkey.

Not bad, she often thought, for a girl who'd moved to Brisbane two years ago at a rather traumatic time in her life.

And now, at twenty-six, she'd had four years of practising as a fully-fledged physiotherapist, and, yes, it was true, she was beginning to make her mark in accident rehabilitation therapy.

She credited this with a genuine love of her job, plus the fact that she was "fancy-free", to use an old-fashioned term, so she could give it her all.

Why she was fancy-free was something she rarely thought about these days. Her life was pleasant, she was able to take overseas holidays and she spent what free time she had doing things she enjoyed. She played golf, she was a movie buff and she belonged to a gourmet cooking club. Her social life wasn't exactly a whirlwind, but she had a circle of friends she saw regularly.

That it should all come crashing down, that pleasant life, the same evening Finn McLeod had put his troublesome business proposition to her, seemed to be the height of irony, but that was what happened.

She juggled her purchases, her bag and the mail she'd retrieved, while she unlocked her door.

She got inside and dropped the mail. She left it on the floor while she put her stuff away and brewed herself a cup of tea. Only then did she retrieve the mail and flick through it as she sank down onto the settee.

It was a fine-quality embossed envelope with a Melbourne postmark that caused her heart to sink like a stone. She recognized the handwriting; her sister's. She knew in her bones that it was a wedding invitation.

That was exactly what slipped out as she slit the envelope: a silver and white card plus a handwritten note. The card had the names Dakota and James curved around wedding bells.

The note said:

Sienna, we've finally agreed to do it. For your sake I fought this as hard as I could, please believe me when I say that, but James and I, well, it just wouldn't go away. I know it's short notice but I feel as if I've been dithering for an eternity— please, please could you be happy for us? And PLEASE could you come to the wedding? Not only for me but Mum and Dad, this is tearing them apart too. Love, your sister Dakota.

Sienna let the note flutter to the coffee-table and despite her distress, couldn't help the faint smile that often curved her lips as she thought of their names, Dakota and Sienna. Her parents were self-confessed hippies of days gone by. They'd roamed the world and seen nothing odd about naming their daughters after the places of their conception.

Now, of course, they were pillars of society and would no doubt be planning a society wedding for their younger daughter, Dakota.

She picked up the card and checked the wedding date as well as the venues—yes, definitely society. Of course James Haig was not un-society himself. He was now a successful stockbroker in the family firm, an old and respected name in the business.

But the crux of the matter was that she herself had been all but engaged to James Haig when her sister had come home from a year overseas, and he'd fallen head over heels in love with Dakota.

Sienna closed her eyes and laid her head back wearily. She had no desire to put herself through all the agony of it again, all the unanswered questions—had he ever loved her, what had he really felt for her? All the bitterness she'd felt towards her sister who couldn't help being just, well, Dakota and enchanting.

Her *younger* sister come to that. Why she should find that galling was an embarrassment to her—what difference did it make to anything? It did, though. On top of being spurned, rejected, on top of the baffling enigma of how close she might have come to marrying a man who didn't love her—how could he have?—it made her feel old and spinsterish.

For crying out aloud, she thought, as some tears slid down her cheeks, she'd even given them her blessing and retreated gracefully. Yes, perhaps it was a self-imposed exile that might have hurt Dakota, had certainly hurt her parents, but what more could she have done? And now they expected her to go to the wedding…

Her mobile phone rang. She checked the number— her mother. I should have expected that, she thought, and was tempted to leave the call unanswered, but in the end she didn't. There was no point, she was going to have to discuss it with one or the other of them some time.

'Hi, Mum! How's it going? I've just got the wedding invitation.' She crossed her fingers. 'I'm really happy for James and Dakota but, look…' she paused and found her eyes drawn to the date on the invitation rather like a magnet '…unfortunately I'll be away on a cattle station out west with a patient.'

Ten minutes later she put down the phone and hugged herself distraughtly.

Her mother had given her to understand that it would

break Dakota's heart if she didn't attend the wedding, not to mention her parents' hearts.

What about my heart? Sienna asked herself. What about the fact that I'd fully expected to be married now and maybe starting a family with a man I—I thought I was head over heels in love with?

On the other hand, why do I feel so *bad* about refusing to go to this wedding? About using a trumped-up excuse—I have no intention of burying myself on a cattle station with Finn McLeod, do I?

Her phone rang again. She snatched it up and was about to turn it off when she saw the number—her boss, the senior partner of the consultancy she worked for, Peter Bannister.

Well, she wanted to talk to him, didn't she? 'Hello, Peter,' she said rather crisply. 'What can I do for you?'

'Sienna, how are you? Look—' he didn't wait for a reply '—I would really take it as a favour if you agreed to go to Waterford with Finn McLeod…'

Five minutes later Sienna ended the call and stared at the phone with an inclination to scream with frustration.

Peter Bannister, it turned out, was a friend of the McLeod family. He'd been away on extended leave, otherwise he would have taken on Finn's rehabilitation himself. By the time he'd returned, he'd reassured himself that Sienna was coping admirably so he'd decided to let things stand. But now, he'd said, he could sense that Finn was really frustrated—it often happened even though the end might be in sight—and he needed a change of scene.

Peter had then gone on to enumerate the virtues of Waterford. Don't expect a tin shack, it's anything but, it even has a nine hole golf course—did you know Finn was a keen golfer before the accident?

Yes, she did, they'd often talked golf.

Well, then, Peter had continued, the Augathella Hospital could use her temporary services, he could arrange a locum situation and those outback areas were often crying out for health professionals.

Then he'd added what he obviously thought was a humorous little bit about how suited she was to do this—no hubby, no kids, no bedridden mums or dads, no pets so far as he knew, only pot-plants and they could be looked after—and that there was no one else in the practice as equally unencumbered. She was the only one who could do it, in other words.

Sienna, at the end of it, had swallowed several times and refused to allow herself to burst into tears. There was no way Peter could know the dreadful irony of what he'd said at this precise moment in her life.

Then she'd opened her mouth to say that she detected the heavy hand of Finn McLeod at work, which actually annoyed the life out of her, but she hadn't said it.

She'd promised to think it over.

This time she sat back exhaustedly as she put the phone down—and tried to think it over.

Peter Bannister was far too ethical to hold it against her if she didn't go. But he'd been very good to her in lots of ways. He'd been happy to be available when she'd needed professional advice. Come to that his wife, Melissa, had found her this apartment and they'd both taken her under their wing while she found her feet in Brisbane. For Peter's sake, she'd like to do it but…

Of course, she could always do both, she thought suddenly. Surely there could be no objection to her taking a weekend off to go to her sister's wedding?

It just so happens I don't want to do either, she thought miserably. Yes, I like Finn, as much as I know him—how well do I know him?

Not a lot, really, she conceded.

Because just as much as she'd kept certain barriers up, kept things professional between them, she'd been helped by the fact that he'd had his own barriers.

Yes, they'd talked golf, they'd talked about all sorts of things in the hours she'd worked with him and encouraged him, but it had all been surface stuff. She had not run into this kind of brick wall side of him. This determination to get his own way.

Perhaps I should have guessed it, though, she reflected with a grimace. His progress *has* been little short of amazing. Maybe I should have realized what kind of personality lay behind that tremendous will-power?

As for her sister's wedding, surely she'd killed all hope stone-dead that it was going to blow over and James would come back to her?

She wouldn't have him back, anyway.

But—she closed her eyes and put her knuckles to her mouth—had her mother and her sister no conception of what it would be like to appear at the wedding amongst a lot of people who, no doubt, knew the background? To be the recipient of curious glances, to have to pretend that she didn't care, she was over it, she wished them happy.

Do they think it will bring me closure? she wondered. Do they think we *are* a family—we used to be a really happy family—and that's paramount? Do they even think I need a catalyst of some kind to help me put it all behind me? Heaven alone knows, they could be right!

But, on top of all that, and this is really trivial, but it's still a barb I can't ignore, do they understand how hard it will be to do while I'm still single and unattached? On the shelf, in other words.

She rubbed her face and thought with a tinge of black humour—maybe I could hire an escort? But where does one find a truly impressive escort? Otherwise it could be worse than being alone…

The name that sprang to mind caused her mouth to drop open and her eyes almost to stand out on stalks.

No, she thought immediately. Oh, no—she even laughed a little and told herself not to be stupid as she knocked the idea stone-cold.

The next morning, however, when it popped up again, she told herself she'd been press-ganged and goaded enough into making her own terms without even stopping to think how it could backfire on her. And that was the only reason she'd allowed it see the light of day.

CHAPTER TWO

'COME to a decision, Sienna?'

They were in Finn's study at Eastwood. They hadn't had their session yet—he'd been delayed so Walt had shown her into the study and provided coffee.

Finn had just put the phone down and he continued, 'I really need to know today.' That, and his earlier question, were the first words he'd spoken to her.

They eyed each other. While she was wearing a track suit and joggers he was more formally dressed in navy trousers and a blue and white pin-striped shirt. He looked every inch a powerful businessman; he didn't look to be in a good mood.

'Why? What difference does a day or two make?' Sienna replied. 'Incidentally—hi! How are you?'

'I'm sorry, that wasn't very polite,' he acknowledged. 'But I have quite a bit on my plate today,' he added briefly.

'So do I. Obviously not the weight of the McLeod empire, but enough.'

Those dark blue eyes narrowed on her as Finn

McLeod took in the shadows beneath her eyes, indicative of a miserably sleepless night.

'Aren't you well?' he asked abruptly. 'You know, a break on a cattle station could do you the world of good. Or…' he paused significantly '…are you such an all-luxury-dependent city girl, the country terrifies you?' There was a wealth of derision in his eyes.

She drew a tumultuous breath, exhaled audibly, then said quite calmly, 'No, it doesn't. However, you're not the only one with an agenda, Finn. I have my own so I'm prepared to bargain with you. I'll come to Waterford if you'll agree to be my escort to my sister's wedding.'

Her first reaction when she'd finished speaking was, Got you, Finn McLeod!—as his jaw dropped and he stared at her incredulously.

Her next reaction was—what had she been thinking? What had she done?

He closed his mouth and said, 'I think you better explain.'

She went hot and cold. Colour flooded her cheeks, then left her looking pale and mortified. 'I—uh—disregard that, Finn, it—sort of came out in the heat of the moment and—'

'No. Tell me, Sienna,' he ordered.

She swallowed and wished herself a million miles away.

'Sienna,' he warned, 'I won't let up until you do.'

She closed her eyes frustratedly, then sighed and told him as clinically as she could. It was only at the end of her explanation that she got emotional.

She said, 'Funnily enough, I don't want to be estranged from my family, I do want Dakota to be happy but the final humiliation—' sudden tears blurred her eyes '—would be to be there amongst them on my own and still, obviously, on the shelf.'

He hadn't interrupted once and all he said when she pulled out a hanky and blew her nose was, 'Dakota?'

Sienna smiled shakily and explained. 'As kids we used to thank our lucky stars we weren't conceived in Timbuktu or Harare. We had a whole alphabet of weird place names we could have ended up with.'

'I see what you mean.' He looked humorous, then sobered. 'But why me?'

'When this bizarre thought literally popped into my head,' she said ruefully, 'that maybe I should hire an escort, my next thought was that it would have to be someone really impressive otherwise it could even be worse!' She shrugged. 'I couldn't, at that moment, come up with anyone more impressive than you. But I never intended to—' She stopped.

'So what do you think made you say it?'

She stared at him and a little flame kindled in her eyes as she forgot about herself and thought about him.

'Finn, you've been really high-handed and arrogant about this. You've gone to my boss behind my back, he's been on the phone to me and the net result is that I'll feel bad if I don't do this on *his* account, not yours, but all the same,' she insisted, 'so—you've even gone to the Augathella Hospital behind my back!'

He looked amused.

'All right, maybe that's not so serious—' she waved

an exasperated hand '—but you have been extremely manipulative and I got *mad* but—'

'I'll come.'

'But—' Sienna stopped as if shot. 'Oh, look, I don't know if that's a good idea. I mean, it sounded all very well, throwing down my own gauntlet in the heat of the moment, but that's essentially what it was.'

'Sienna,' he said dangerously, 'let's keep it simple—if you come to Waterford, I'll go to the wedding with you.'

'But—'

'Sienna,' he growled.

'All right. Thank you. I mean—' her shoulders slumped '—at least you've made my mother's day.'

'Why?' she said suddenly about an hour later.

They were in the pool doing floatation exercises.

It was a warm, muggy Brisbane day; the humidity of semi-tropical Brisbane was something Sienna wondered if she'd ever get used to. So it was pleasant to be in the pool surrounded by the gardens of Eastwood.

She wore a hat and dark glasses and a sleek navy Speedo. She was anointed with sunscreen, and she'd broken off her instructions suddenly to ask her question.

Finn lay suspended in the fluorescent blue water on his back, then he flipped over and paddled to the side. He pushed his wet hair out of his eyes and studied her for a long moment. 'You may not want to know why.'

'Yes, I do,' she insisted.

He shrugged. His shoulders were broad and tanned and powerful and the only blemishes on his body were several scars from the accident and the operations he had had to have on his leg—in that respect he'd been amazingly lucky, no facial scars at all. 'It all sounded rather like a cry for help.'

Sienna flinched.

'It also sounded as if you had no one else to call on. Being dumped in favour of your little sister would no doubt account for that, although isn't two years a fair while to be carrying a torch?'

'In two years' time, you may find you have to ask yourself that same question, Finn,' she said quietly.

'*Touché.*' He rubbed his jaw. 'Well, something like that. Incidentally, I had been advised you had no ties and seemed determined to stay that way, so I wasn't quite as high-handed as you imagined.'

Sienna sank down to her sunglasses and came up spluttering. 'Peter, I suppose!' she said indignantly.

He nodded.

Sienna said something highly uncomplimentary as she called the wrath of God down on Peter Bannister, all men for that matter, and possibly even Melissa Bannister with her kind but gossipy ways.

'If you're imagining I'm all droopy and sad, I'm not.'

'No.' He shook his head and his lips quirked. 'The opposite if anything. A bundle of energy and intelligence, actually. But I can't help wondering if you see yourself as turned off men for the duration?' There was something curiously intent in the way he watched her.

'Yes and no,' she said slowly. 'I guess, as much as anything, it's my own judgement that's a bit of a worry.' She smiled humourlessly and rippled the surface of the water with her fingers. 'Then again, while you obviously can't condemn all men because of one man's erratic emotions, to be honest—' this time her smile was genuine although wry '—it's hard not to sometimes.'

'So have you thought about the rest of your life in this context? Marriage? Children?'

Sienna bit her lip. 'Yes,' she said quietly. 'I love kids, I think I've done some of my best work with children, but I can't see myself falling madly in love again so—' she looked away and her voice was a little clogged as she went on '—I don't know.'

'Where is this wedding and when?'

She told him. 'You should, at the rate you're going, be pretty mobile.'

'Glory be,' he said dryly.

'Look,' Sienna said carefully, 'I feel really bad now, Finn. I mean, a wedding, after—after what happened to you, might be the last thing you want to go to.' She stopped and sighed. 'I just didn't think. So I'll come to Waterford but you don't have to come to the wedding— I'd quite understand.'

'Sienna—' his eyes were laughing at her although he spoke gravely '—you surprise me. I would never have taken you for such a mass of indecision.'

'I'm not, usually.' She took her hat off, splashed some water on her head and repositioned the hat. 'My mother rang me yesterday—that's really wheeling in the heavy guns—and I don't seem to have known if I was on my head or my heels ever since!'

He laughed openly. 'I'll come.'

'Are you sure?' She eyed him anxiously.

'I'm sure.'

Sienna pulled herself out of the pool, entirely unaware, as she had her back to him, how he studied her sleek slender figure as water streamed off her. Then she turned round and planted her hands on her hips.

'But…' she began—and couldn't go on as she realized she seemed to be under a rather particular scrutiny from her patient.

And indeed, high, perfect little breasts with delicious peaks, Finn McLeod found himself thinking as he gazed up at her, not to mention those tantalizing hips. What kind of a mix would his no-nonsense physiotherapist with that desirable figure be in bed?

'But…' Sienna said again—and again couldn't seem to go on.

Finn grimaced and swam out into the middle of the pool. 'I am coming to your sister's wedding, Ms Torrance, that's final.'

Sienna decided not to call her mother that night. She still couldn't quite believe Finn McLeod would accompany her to Dakota's wedding, or that she should let him. So she thought she'd wait a day or two before breaking the news. She was still curiously perturbed by those moments beside the pool when she'd completely lost the thread of what she'd been going to say!

Her mother had other ideas, however. She rang Sienna from a private line so the number wasn't displayed on the mobile screen.

Sienna answered a bit distractedly as she cooked a pasta dish for her dinner. 'Hello, Sienna Torrance here.'

'I know, darling,' her mother's voice said down the

line. 'I'm afraid I've been a bit sneaky. This is not my phone. I didn't want you to know it was me in case you didn't want to talk to me.'

'Mum—' Sienna felt a shaft of guilt as she put the phone on its stand and turned on the loudspeaker '—of course not.' She drizzled the pasta with garlic butter and freshly chopped herbs. 'I—'

'But I just wanted to tell you again that I know it would be difficult for you to come to the wedding. *Please* don't think I—*we're* being thoughtless and only thinking of Dakota, although she is miserable and—'

'Mum,' Sienna broke in as she scooped some pine nuts into her pasta, 'it's OK. I've been able to get a weekend off for the wedding, but could I bring someone with me?'

'Who?'

'Well, a friend—'

'A man?'

'Yes, he is.' Sienna deployed a pasta spoon on the mixture.

'Oh, my darling,' her mother breathed, 'of course you can! Who is he? Tell me about him. You haven't ever mentioned him, but you must know him pretty well if you want to bring him to Dakota's wedding! Is he nice? Of course he would be! Is he good-looking?'

Sienna abandoned the spoon and closed her eyes. 'Mum, we're just...friends.'

'What's his name?'

Sienna hesitated, then said reluctantly, 'Finn McLeod.'

'Not—not *those* McLeods?'

'Yes, but—now listen to me, Mum, I don't want you to tell a soul otherwise I won't come. It's—we're just friends.'

'Your secret is perfectly safe with me,' her mother said with a tinge of reproach, but added immediately, 'That's wonderful news. I'm so happy for you! Oh, darling, I have to go, I borrowed this mobile phone and it's blinking red lights at me now. I think the battery may be going but we'll talk soon…'

Her mother's voice faded away.

Sienna switched off her phone, then banged her head against the corkboard on the kitchen wall, twice.

How could her pleasant if uneventful life have turned into such a minefield in the space of twenty-four hours?

I'll tell you, she told herself grimly. Pride. And little white lies.

Then she sniffed and realized her pasta was burning. She turned the plate off, pushed the pan away, suddenly not hungry in the slightest. She poured herself a glass of white wine, which she took outside onto the balcony.

Dusk was drawing in and it was cooler but still humid. A family of squeakers, raucous, bright-eyed, inquisitive little birds, was settling down in a grevillea tree that clung to the slope below the building. The creamy cone-shaped grevillea flower heads with their delicate tendrils glowed almost candlelike in the gathering gloom.

But what occupied her mind was the distinct possibility that Finn McLeod could shortly find his name linked to one Sienna Torrance, whether he liked it or not.

So what do I do about that? she wondered.

Well, it's obvious, isn't it? I have to nip this in the bud. No more pride, no more little white lies, and the sooner the better.

* * *

It was Walt who admitted her to Eastwood an hour later and showed her into the den.

Finn was sitting on a settee watching cricket on a large-screen television. There was a coffee-pot and two cups on a table in front of him. He wore a white cotton shirt and cargo pants. His cane was leaning against the settee beside him.

'Sienna,' he murmured in a way that she couldn't identify as welcoming or unwelcoming—actually quite noncommittal, she decided, and flinched inwardly.

He also took his time about looking her over.

She'd changed after making the phone call to ask if she could come and see him, into a silky lemon blouse tucked into indigo jeans. Her hair, straight and shoulder-length and usually tied back in a pony-tail, was loose and naturally streaked light and darker honey-gold, and held back by a silver slide on one side.

For some reason, his appraisal of her caused her to look down at herself, but she couldn't see anything wrong with her outfit and she looked up and into his eyes with a faint frown.

He shrugged. 'It's the first time I've seen you out of track suits, swimmers and pony-tails. You scrub up well.'

She blinked and a ghost of humour lit his eyes.

'Believe me,' he murmured.

'I—thank you. So do you, for that matter.' She drew a deep breath. 'Finn, I'm really sorry about coming to see you like this, but it is Friday, so I wouldn't have seen you until Monday in the normal course of events and it wouldn't be easy to do over the phone.'

'That's OK. Sit down and pour the coffee,' he invited. 'Something's come up?' he hazarded.

'Yes, my mother,' Sienna said exasperatedly and poured the coffee before she went on, sitting adjacent to him in an armchair. 'Please believe me when I say I love my mother dearly, but this is what happened.' And she recounted the recent conversation she'd had with her mother.

At the end he raised an eyebrow and said, 'So?'

'Well, not only is she convinced—because it's what she wants to believe!—that you and I are—' She paused.

'Lovers?' he suggested.

'Oh, well—oh, well, on the way to it anyway—' Sienna looked discomforted '—but—only in her happiness for me!—it's quite possible she won't be able to keep it a secret.'

Finn sat up and reached for his coffee-cup, but before he took a sip he said, with obvious amusement, 'What a tangled web we weave—and I guess you know the rest of it.'

'Exactly,' Sienna responded with some urgency. 'And because it's *you*, it could get out of hand. The press could get onto it. Come to that, even without my mother—why didn't I think of this sooner?—just your being at the wedding with me could spark all sorts of speculation!'

'How terrifying,' he remarked, causing Sienna to blink at him again.

'You mean you—wouldn't mind?' She stared at him, round-eyed.

'I never take any notice of the press in those circumstances,' he drawled. 'Besides, isn't that the object of the exercise—to have your family and friends of the opinion you aren't on the shelf?'

'But—after what happened to you—and it's not that long ago…' She stopped and steepled her fingertips, rapping them together lightly. 'I really don't feel I could do that to you.'

He watched her tapping fingers for a moment. 'Well, I appreciate that, Sienna,' he said almost lazily, 'but you don't have to worry about me. I can take care of myself.'

Sienna discovered herself to be counting beneath her breath, but she'd only got to three when she burst out frustratedly, 'What do I have to do to get you *not* to come to this wedding?'

'If you hadn't brought it up in the first place, that might have helped. Besides, you've been a real inspiration to me, and it seems like one small way I could repay you.'

She opened her mouth, but closed it because nothing—coherent at least—would come out.

'Anyway,' Finn McLeod continued reasonably, 'do you want this family turmoil of yours to continue?'

'No, of course not—' She broke off abruptly.

'Do you want him back?'

'No! Definitely not!'

'Then this is one way to get a reunion over and done with. It's one way to allow your sister to ride off happily into the sunset.'

'But it's a farce all the same!'

'You know, my dear…' he paused and studied her thoughtfully '…sometimes sticking to the straight and narrow truth-wise may be all very well—but it can also be a kind of self-righteousness that's self-defeating.'

She gazed at him with her lips parted.

He smiled faintly. 'You don't want him back, you don't want to be at odds with your family, you particularly don't want to feel like a wall-flower at this wedding so—'

'Don't go on,' Sienna interrupted stiffly.

He grimaced and rubbed his jaw.

'I feel awful now,' she continued. 'Really awful. Proud, insufferably priggish—'

He laughed aloud. 'Sienna, it was your idea in the first place! I'm just telling you I think it was a good one and a fitting exchange for all you've done for me.'

'I—see.' She couldn't think of anything else to say.

'So it's a deal? No more doubts?'

'It's a deal,' she said slowly.

In bed that night, Sienna found she was puzzled.

She and Finn had finished their coffee companionably as they'd watched the cricket, an exciting one-day international match. In fact so companionable had it been, she'd stayed to the end of the match.

But, as the overhead fan revolved above her bed, she found herself trying to sum Finn McLeod up in the light of recent events, only to decide he was still something of an enigma.

Yes, his decision to come to the wedding was a gesture she had to appreciate. Yes, he was good company with a rather dry sense of humour that she appreciated. Yes, she'd certainly spent a lot of time with him over the last few months so they did have a rapport of a kind and she was able to read him in some ways.

For example, although they didn't happen often, she'd learnt to identify his bad days just by looking at him. Days when he was pale and moody, haunted almost—and who wouldn't be after what he'd gone through? And she'd adjusted her responses accordingly to purely businesslike.

But it was hard to shake the feeling that he was—how to describe it?—a cool customer, and despite the quid pro quo he'd agreed to as a way of repaying her for what she'd done for him, why did she still feel there was something going on she didn't understand?

She reached above her and turned the fan to a higher speed, and closed her eyes as the faster air wafted over her skin. She did have an air-conditioning unit but she hated sleeping with the windows closed and in the air-conditioning.

What on earth *could* be going on, though? she wondered. And why did she have this feeling? Because she had genuinely thought, when she'd stopped to think about it, that a wedding would be the last thing he'd want to go to after his own wedding plans had been so tragically destroyed.

Because, she mused, she *had* thought that to have his name linked to another woman, even falsely, should not appeal to him after those same tragic events.

Yet he'd been totally relaxed about it all. Or did that mean Finn McLeod had shut himself off, put his emotions on ice, in other words, because it was the only way he could cope?

* * *

Finn had no reservations about taking advantage of air-conditioning to get a good night's sleep, but even in the cool, climate-controlled atmosphere of the master bedroom of Eastwood he was having trouble sleeping that night.

Of course, there was something else he could take advantage of, a sleeping pill, but he had grave reservations about becoming dependent on them, so he didn't.

And things were improving. The pain in his leg was gradually diminishing, he was getting more and more mobile, the terrible tearing, crashing nightmares were less frequent.

The twisted remains of his life were another matter, however.

And there was this mysterious urge he'd succumbed to, to force his physiotherapist to come to Waterford with him.

His lips twisted as he recalled Sienna's desperate indecision after flinging down her own gauntlet in the heat of the moment. But, if anything, it reinforced his belief that she was a thoroughly nice person.

She was also attractive in her own quiet way. She was certainly capable, intelligent and, as he'd told her, a bundle of energy. She was pleasant company.

Did that justify his behaviour, though?

He stirred restlessly. It was true that he was feeling frustrated and needed a change of scene. It was true enough that he thought she'd worked wonders for him whatever she might like to think to the contrary, although it was hard to pinpoint exactly how she'd done it. A born carer? he wondered. With a knack for people and a passion for getting them moving again? Possibly.

So why was he feeling guilty now?

It made sense for him not to want to swap horses mid-stream, so to speak, but was that all that was behind it?

Sienna continued her work with Finn throughout the next week, and discovered again that he could be "difficult", as she thought of it.

It all came about over her refusal—at first, that was—to agree to him discarding his stick.

They finished their session in the gym—a late session as it happened, to fit in with a meeting he'd had earlier—but he refused point-blank to be pushed back to the house in his chair.

'I've also decided I don't need the stick any more,' he stated.

'Finn, don't be silly!' She stared at him.

'You said that to me once before, but there was nothing silly about that either,' he countered, his eyes dark and moody again. 'Have you any idea what it feels like to be tottering around on a stick? Or pushed about by a slip of a girl?'

'Of course I do! Not that it matters who does the pushing, I would have thought!'

'Yes, it does,' he stated. 'It makes me feel about a hundred years old and useless.'

Sienna took a breath and counted to three. 'You'd probably really feel a hundred years old if you fell over and broke something. All right—' she came to a sudden decision '—no more chair but it's quite—quite childish to do away with your stick.' She drew herself up to her full five feet six inches and stared at him with the authority she seldom had to use with patients.

It didn't work.

He grinned fleetingly and said quite gently, 'Ms Torrance, you may insult me all you like, but you cannot stop me.' He turned away and started to walk out.

Sienna muttered something beneath her breath as she watched his retreating figure, then, 'I can take myself off your case, *Mr McLeod*, which would mean you'd have to find someone else to go to Waterford with you.'

He stopped, then turned back. 'Fighting words, my dear, but what about your sister Dakota's wedding?'

Sienna opened her mouth and closed it.

'Especially in light of not only having told them you're bringing someone but who?'

Several emotions chased through Sienna's eyes. 'I—well, I'd just have to swallow my pride, that's all.'

He surveyed her, then his lips quirked. 'How about swallowing your pride and conceding this? I could be the best judge of the stick bit.'

'Why?'

'I'll tell you over dinner.'

'Dinner! Here? No. Thank you, but no,' she amended.

'We've been down this road before,' he commented. 'All the same, you choose then.'

'Choose?' she repeated, looking bewildered.

He shrugged. 'You seemed to suggest *here* was the problem. That's fine with me, so how about some neutral territory?'

Sienna drew several breaths of varying intensity,

frustration being the dominant emotion they signified. 'That's twisting my words!'

'Not as you said them. Don't you want to know why I'm of a mind to do away with my stick, Sienna?'

'And that's twisting my arm,' she retorted.

'I know a rather nice restaurant on the river,' he remarked with his eyes full of amusement. 'Their lobster and Moreton Bay bugs are amazing.'

Sienna opened her mouth and closed it. If she had one weakness it was fresh seafood and Moreton Bay bugs came at the top of that list. 'Well,' she said rather weakly, then eyed him accusingly. 'How did you know that?'

He lifted an eyebrow enquiringly.

'That I would sell my soul for Moreton Bay bugs.' She shook her head exasperatedly.

He grinned. 'I didn't, but I like the sound of that.'

'If you think I'm a pushover in any other direction, think again!' she warned.

'Perish the thought,' he murmured, then laughed at her expression. 'Sienna, I'm only asking you to have dinner with me.'

She exhaled audibly. 'All right. Just this once. But I need to go home and change.'

'Not a problem.' He glanced at his watch. 'Give me your address and Dave and I will pick you up at, say, seven?'

Sienna drove home, still seething inwardly, but once there she went into another mode.

She showered and changed into a swirly, silky three-quarter-length skirt, a white background with a cinnamon pattern on it and a white knit top. She slid her feet into bronze sandals and looped her hair up into a loose knot.

She applied some discreet make-up, then studied herself in the mirror and decided that her upswept hair called for some dangly earrings. She found a pair, tiny seed pearls on copper wire, and put them on.

Then she stood quite still and asked herself why she was going out of her way to look her best when she'd been literally conned into this dinner.

Because that's what Finn McLeod does to you, she conceded with a little spark of fire in her eyes. Puts you on your mettle even when you're extremely annoyed with him!

Well, she conceded, annoyed with him and herself—you could have said no!

Dave knocked on her door at seven exactly and escorted her down to the waiting, latest model Mercedes. She climbed into the back, Finn was in the front, and she breathed in the scent of fine new leather.

But to her immediate consternation she saw that Finn was wearing a suit, although no tie.

'Uh—what kind of restaurant are we going to?' she asked as Dave drove them off.

'Angelo's,' Finn replied.

Sienna clicked her tongue. Angelo's was one of Brisbane's most exclusive restaurants.

Finn turned his head towards her. 'Is that a problem?'

'I'm not dressed for Angelo's. I'm dressed,' Sienna said with precision, 'for a rather nice restaurant on the river—which to me indicated somewhere casual and

pleasant rather than five-star and extremely up-market.'
Her voice had risen a little.

'I don't see anything wrong with the way you're
dressed, but, to set your mind at rest, I've booked a
table on the deck—it *is* more casual than the main restaurant.'

'How on earth did you get a table—even on the
deck—at such short notice?'

'They know me.'

'Silly question,' Sienna muttered to herself, but any
further utterances were forestalled as Dave drew up
opposite the striped awning that protected the famous
green brass-handled front doors of Angelo's.

Sienna had never been to the restaurant but she'd
heard of it; not only exquisite cuisine but one of *the*
places to be seen in town.

The rumours hadn't lied, she saw immediately. The
décor was fabulous. Burgundy walls, champagne
marble floors, soft, concealed lighting and forest-green
velvet upholstery upon pale beech chairs. That pale
glossy wood was repeated in the grand piano being
played softly in the background.

And her eyes nearly popped at the number of celeb-
rities she recognized. Not only that, but it was a glitter-
ing throng dressed to the nines, as Finn was greeted with
reverence and ushered towards the deck. He was also
stopped delightedly several times by other guests, at the
same time as she was scanned from top to toe with a few
raised eyebrows and the odd frown—but then immediate dismissal.

The analogy that sprang to mind had to do with her

earrings. Pretty enough, but how could seed pearls on copper wire compete with the array of South Sea pearls glowing like moons, the diamonds and other gems that were displayed on the necks, ears, wrists and fingers of the female clientele of Angelo's? Ditto her pretty but relatively inexpensive, definitely not designer outfit.

She set her teeth and raised her chin as they walked through to the deck.

It might be more casual than the main restaurant, but the deck was lovely. There were braziers flaming along the roped-off edge, potted palms swaying slightly in a gentle breeze and the crystal and silverware glinted on snowy white cloths.

When they were finally seated at the best table on the deck, with the river flowing past below their feet with reflected lights bobbing on its surface, she said, 'Very impressive, Mr McLeod,' but with an edge to her voice.

He eyed her narrowly. 'Something tells me you don't approve?'

'Oh, I have no doubt I'll approve of the bugs.' She gestured. 'I just feel a little out of place.'

He looked genuinely surprised. 'Why?'

'Everyone looks like a millionaire, if not to say a billionaire or a celebrity—' she glanced around '—even on the deck. As for the prices—' she glanced at the menu she'd been handed '—they're little short of daylight robbery.'

'Isn't…' He paused. 'Couldn't you be indulging in an inverted form of snobbery, Sienna?'

'Well, actually, I'm all for quality, but I'm also a value-for-money girl. I could have taken you to a place where they do divine bugs for half the price, and the ambience isn't bad either.'

He stared at her.

'This is not exactly my milieu, Finn,' she added gently. 'It's like another world, your world. It's—' she looked around '—very glamorous but a little bit false.'

'I stand corrected,' he said gravely. 'Shall we go to your restaurant?'

Sienna's eyes widened. 'You mean stand up and walk out?'

He shrugged. 'Why not?'

She blinked. 'What will they think?'

'Does it matter?'

It came to Sienna at that moment that this was the essence of being super-wealthy. Not only paying inflated prices for being surrounded by your peers and being seen on the social scene, but doing precisely as you pleased, and Finn McLeod did it in spades.

'Er—no,' she said. 'I would feel bad, only on behalf of the staff, about doing that.'

'So you're happy to grin and bear it?' he suggested.

'I—I'll tell you how I feel after I've sampled the bugs.'

She looked at him coolly until he smiled with genuine amusement.

'You're quite a character, Miss Torrance,' he murmured. 'Tell me this—do you drink?'

'Of course I drink.'

'I mean as in wine? Something light and refreshing to go with the seafood, maybe?'

'Why not? Do I look like a teetotaller?' she asked wryly.

'I just thought, having been castigated on the

excesses of this place, that might be another of your pet aversions.'

Sienna grimaced. 'Sorry, perhaps I got a bit carried away—it's a little demoralizing to feel under-dressed, in case you hadn't realized.'

'My apologies. The last thing I wanted to do was embarrass you, but there is no need—you look absolutely fine.'

Sienna chewed her lip. He sounded as if he meant it. Perhaps it simply hadn't crossed his mind that you needed to give a girl fair warning before you took her to Angelo's? Maybe the women he normally escorted around expected no less?

'Thank you, I'll rise above it then—and I'd love some wine to go with the seafood.'

'Bravo!' His eyes lingered on her for a long moment but were entirely enigmatic, before he turned away to order the wine.

A couple of hours later, crispy, garlic-butter-soaked bread and tapas had come and gone as well as melt-in-the-mouth barbecued bugs on a bed of rice with a green salad. And Sienna realized—how had he done it?—they hadn't talked about his stick at all. If anything, they'd mostly talked about her.

Somehow, maybe the wine had helped, he'd broken through her barriers of resentment and feelings of ill-use and got her to talk about herself. Her university days, her passion for her career, her travels, even her politics!

'How did you do that?' she asked him out of the blue.

He raised an eyebrow.

'Invite me to dinner to talk about your stick, then get me to talk about anything but?'

He shrugged. 'Most people love talking about themselves.'

'Yes, but I'm usually—' She gestured. 'Things are usually the other way around for me. I'm the one who does the asking.'

'I've noticed that. You're very good at making light, unimportant conversation.'

'Just like a hairdresser,' she said mischievously.

'What do people tell you?' he asked curiously.

She raised her eyes heavenwards. 'The most amazing things sometimes. Quite often things I'd rather not know.' She smiled ruefully, then sobered. 'But—why?'

'I guess—' he put his napkin on the table '—I'm interested, that's all. As for my stick, if you really want to know, I think it's holding me back mentally now.'

She frowned. 'What do you mean?'

'I need a new challenge. I need to throw it away. Of course it goes without saying I'll be careful.' He frowned suddenly. 'It's like a prop and it's annoying me to think I need a prop. I don't know if that makes sense, but there you go.'

'So,' she said slowly, 'whatever I say is not going to make any difference?'

He shook his head.

She considered. 'I know what you mean in a way. I took up ice-skating as a kid. I was scared stiff to leave the rail for ages. Then I realized the rail was actually holding me back. But—' she looked at him intently '—there's much more at stake here, Finn. You're a big man—you could fall hard. Promise me you'll take it very easily.'

'I promise.' He looked at his watch. 'Dave will be here shortly to pick us up. Thank you for a very pleasant evening, Sienna.'

She sat back. 'May I tell you something?'

His eyes narrowed. 'Yes.'

'I don't—' She hesitated and stared out over the river. 'I still don't entirely understand what's going on.'

'As in?' he queried.

She thought carefully, then said bluntly, 'Do you have an agenda I'm not aware of?'

He looked reflective. 'Yes, I do have an agenda, well, I have one agenda—above all, you could say. I want to be fighting fit again. That's why I need you to come to Waterford, Sienna, and—to be in accord with the decision, not as if you've been given no choice.'

I suppose that makes sense, she mused, and looked at him rather helplessly. There was no doubt she'd enjoyed the dinner and his company. She supposed she *was* now feeling happier about it all.

He pushed his chair back and they stood up.

And it hit her from nowhere that he was almost impossibly tall, dark and handsome, a magnetic presence that caused her skin to prickle as they faced each other. And the prickle became a flood of awareness of all the finer points of Finn McLeod.

The tanned column of his throat rising from his white shirt was tantalizing, as were the lines of his shoulders beneath the beautifully tailored grey suit—she was hit by a sudden vision of them when he wore his swimming trunks, sleek and powerful, as was his torso with its thick line of dark hair running from his navel downwards...

She took an unexpected breath as she felt her pulses riot and looked into his eyes—to disturb an all-encompassing glance from him that seemed to be taking an awful lot of her in. From her slender neck and the pretty dangly earrings, from her breasts beneath the white cotton top to her reed-slim waist and the flare of her hips.

But just as she was moved to wonder incredulously whether he was experiencing the same kind of tingly moment that she was he looked away and said casually, 'After you, ma'am!'

She blinked, to clear her mind and her vision. She was obviously mistaken—about him—and she had to be mistaken about the feeling that told her she would not be able to resist Finn if—if...

She refused to allow that "if" to be quantified even in her mind. Because many women probably got "tingly" moments in his company, but he was just a man after all. A difficult one at times too, she reminded herself dryly, but, above all, he was a patient.

'OK,' she said with decision, 'I'll put my heart and soul into coming to Waterford, if that's what was worrying you. I would have anyway.'

He smiled curiously austerely and said only, 'Thank you.'

But Sienna was annoyed, she discovered. Annoyed and keyed up and unable to break the spell of Finn McLeod, let alone face the walk through the main restaurant under so many curious eyes, she had no doubt.

She swallowed and counted to three beneath her

breath—why did she never get past three?—then turned and walked away quite unaware that her state of mind had induced an annoyed, proud, hip-swinging walk.

She had absolutely no idea that Finn McLeod watched her precede him, and found himself wondering what it would be like to view his down-to-earth physiotherapist walk away from him swinging her unclothed hips.

Sienna sat on her veranda with a cup of lemon tea before going to bed.

She was perplexed; she was uneasy about her reaction to Finn. It was all very well to class herself with a whole lot of faceless women who might react similarly to him, but was it realistic?

On the other hand what future could there ever be for her with Finn McLeod?

In hindsight it amazed her that she'd felt so out of place at the restaurant. There was little class distinction in Australian society, or so she'd thought. She'd believed she could take her place anywhere, yet she'd got the distinct feeling at Angelo's that she'd entered the world of the mega-rich and famous, and, not only was it ultra-glamorous and expensive, it was also clannish.

Then again, she thought with a touch of humour, glamorous, gorgeous models were renowned for breaking into that world, weren't they? But there was a vast difference between Sienna Torrance and a top model—or a sparkling, beautiful TV presenter, come to that.

She finished her tea and decided she felt better. Finn McLeod was definitely not for her! All she had to do was hold onto that thought…

CHAPTER THREE

SIENNA'S next surprise came two days before they were due to fly out.

She was invited to dinner at Eastwood, with the Bannisters.

She wasn't that keen on going but if nothing else it provided her with some background to the McLeods, some background to Finn himself, even a touch of humour.

His aunt was the hostess.

His aunt and her mother would make a good pair, Sienna decided.

Not that Finn showed the slightest tendency to allow his aunt, Alice McLeod, to interfere in his life. She was obviously dead set against him going to Waterford and had even bravely offered to go with him despite loathing cattle stations. It obviously still rankled that he'd refused her heroic offer.

There were eight people at the dinner in Eastwood's panelled, candlelit, formal dining room: Finn and his aunt, Peter and Melissa, another couple and Finn's younger half-brother Declan.

While Sienna knew Finn was thirty-six, Declan

was about twenty-eight, she judged. They were also like chalk and cheese, the McLeod brothers, obviously representative of having different mothers. Beside Finn's dark, impressive maturity, Declan was a thin, fair blade of a man whose latest endeavour had been three months on a yacht cruising the islands of French Polynesia.

Sienna summed him up as the playboy of the family, but had to admit he was entertaining.

It turned out to be a pleasant evening with superb food, although Sienna was glad she'd taken Melissa's advice to "dress up". Not that she'd needed it after her experience at Angelo's.

She'd chosen a fitted, short gun-metal dress embroidered with black beads and with shoestring straps. She wore high, pointed black sandals and while she might not have been flashing diamonds and pearls—Alice was radiant with them—her fair skin glowed and her smooth hair shone as it swirled to her shoulders.

She hadn't had to wonder why she'd been invited into this socially elevated circle because it was Alice McLeod who'd issued the invitation by phone. She'd gone on to say that, since Peter and Melissa were coming, Sienna should feel quite at home, and, anyway, she really wanted to get to meet the person who was going to Waterford with Finn.

Sienna hadn't had the presence of mind to decline on the spot, then she'd thought, Why not? At least I might get some idea of what I'm getting into.

She found herself seated between Peter and Declan and opposite Finn; she found herself, increasingly during the evening, fending off subtle overtures from Declan.

She got the feeling Finn was quite aware of what was going on, but, beyond a couple of narrowed little glances from him, she had no idea what he was thinking.

But as seafood chowder was replaced by fillet mignon and crisp vegetables, as that was replaced by a summer berry dessert—strawberries, raspberries and blueberries drizzled with Cointreau and served with home-made ice cream—and the wine flowed, she mostly enjoyed herself.

Alice McLeod was obviously a character. A spinster—she looked anything but—in her early sixties, she was a prominent dietitian with several popular books to her credit. She no longer lived at Eastwood, only Finn lived in the house now, Sienna gathered, and Alice was also a fund-raiser for several charities. She took in good part Declan's observation that it was all a good excuse to have a black and white ball or two.

If she was sizing Sienna up she did it discreetly. Although it did occur to Sienna there might be more to it than checking out her nephew's physiotherapist, but what, she had no idea, until it occurred to her that they did have something in common—they both worked in health.

The conversation was wide-ranging and often witty, but Sienna found herself thinking that Finn looked tired, and she was pleased on his behalf when it broke up relatively early.

It was Finn who saw her to her car—she had adroitly avoided Declan's attempt to do it.

But she said to Finn, who was not using his stick, 'You don't need to see me out, you look—somewhat weary.'

He glanced at her with a tinge of surprise. 'How can you tell?'

'I'm trained for it and I do know you rather well, in that context. Having trouble sleeping?'

'Yes, as a matter of fact, but I'm sure I'll catch up. You didn't appear to take to my brother.'

Sienna grinned and waved a hand. 'He's OK. I don't think he realized he was dealing with an expert, not to mention a girl not quite left at the altar.'

Finn chuckled. 'An expert, though?'

'It's not only confidences I get, I get the most outrageous proposals from men from time to time,' she explained. 'It's an occupational hazard. I've got rejecting them down to a fine art.'

'Ouch,' he murmured.

She grinned. 'Well, thank you for a very nice evening. You know, the habit of not sleeping can also be—be self-defeating.'

'What would you recommend? I refuse to become dependent on sleeping pills.'

'Go for a swim, then, or some gentle exercise in the gym, maybe a massage.'

Finn looked down at her and opened his mouth to tell her he'd tried all of that and none of it had worked for him. But he stopped abruptly as he studied her.

Her shiny head came to just above his shoulder. The gun-metal dress made her skin look particularly creamy and smooth and it emphasized her reed-slim waist. He didn't know if it was the colour of the dress, but her grey eyes, fringed with darker lashes, were wide and clear and rather beautiful. So was the outline of her mouth, severely drawn, but her lips were soft and pink.

And he took a careful breath as it occurred to him just what would work for him.

To have her in his arms in his bed, to be warm and comfortable with her, some idle talk about the dinner party maybe, then a slow, intimate exploration of her body...

How would Sienna Torrance react to that if he put it into words? he wondered. With one of her well-practised put-downs?

He smiled an ironic little smile as he thought of his half-brother Declan, but he sobered abruptly.

Exactly what kind of trouble was he running into with this girl?

'All right,' he said. 'Goodnight.' And he turned away.

Sienna watched him limp away with a question mark in her eyes. Had she just had a door closed in her face, and if so, why?

Two weeks later Sienna was convinced, despite agreeing to go to Waterford with Finn McLeod, that she'd somehow lost her easy camaraderie with him, and it just didn't make sense. Particularly not after their exchange of views when he'd taken her to dinner.

All the same, Waterford had proved quite an experience.

Augathella was seven hundred kilometres north west of Brisbane on the Matilda Highway. The township, sitting alongside the Warrego River, was small and definitely "outback", but it was the nerve centre of the district, often arid country but home to sheep and cattle stations.

Yet only a two hour drive north was Carnarvon Gorge, carved out of the sandstone cliffs of the Great Dividing Range. A place of torrents, cool rocky pools and steep green slopes, it was completely different from the surrounding dusty plains.

They'd flown over the gorge on their way to Waterford and Sienna had been entranced by its beauty.

She'd also been somewhat amazed by the entourage Finn flew to Waterford in his own plane.

His masseur, Dave, and Walt, the butler—she'd discovered that this was a household joke. Walt certainly performed household co-ordination duties, but he didn't look anything like a butler. He was short, thin and middle-aged, he often wore jeans, he was quietly spoken and very capable—and his name was Walter Butler.

Along with Walt and Dave and herself had come Finn's principal private secretary, and two pilots had completed the party.

Then there was Waterford itself. The homestead was over a hundred years old with pale pink walls, sweeping grey roofs, verandas, courtyards and an awful lot of history.

It was beautifully maintained with shining parquet floors, chandeliers, oriental rugs to die for and art, maps and memorabilia on the walls you could spend an age studying.

One of her favourite rooms was the gallery lined with glass-fronted cabinets of semi-precious stones and minerals found in the area: opals, amethysts, sapphires, crystals and gold-speckled rocks. At one end of the gallery was a Wurlitzer pianola, old but in mint condition, and with a bunya pine chest containing dozens of music rolls.

Another room was designated as the games room and held a vast billiard table as well as card tables and a chess set.

All the rooms had fireplaces against the minus-five-degrees winter minimum temperatures. Not that Sienna could visualize five degrees Celsius below in the thirty degrees above of summer, but she did appreciate the lack of humidity in the air.

As for sleeping accommodation, only she and Dave, and Finn, of course, were in the main house. She and Dave each had guest suites; bedrooms with *en suite* bathrooms and a private sitting room.

The rest of the party, all men, slept in a wing of the house called the annexe and separated by a covered walkway, along with the household staff. There was yet more accommodation for guests within the main compound, she was to discover: a four-bedroom cottage known as the Green House.

The gardens were something else Sienna appreciated, in fact they made her thumbs prickle. Thanks to bore water the house environs were ablaze with colour, bougainvillea from white through pink to deep purple, oleanders and agapanthus, frangipani and many more flowering shrubs. The herb garden was a special delight.

She couldn't quibble with the atmosphere at Waterford, which was much more relaxed than Eastwood, she suspected.

They all ate together at a long refectory table in an alcove off the kitchen. They all went their separate ways during the day, but if you wanted companionship during the evening it was there to be had in the games room.

And for a girl who had expressed grave doubts about being buried on a cattle station for weeks, she was having to eat her words.

She found it exciting, she found she loved the wide open spaces, she even got used to the dust in record time. She'd ridden as a child and was happy to be able to do so again when she could borrow a horse.

She was fascinated by the whole set-up of stockmen and boundary riders, the cattle dogs, the marvellously agile stock horses and the more mechanical processes of mustering cattle such as quad bikes and a helicopter; she absorbed it all with a glow that was plain for anyone to see.

Waterford was like a small town, she decided. Outside the main house compound were several staff cottages and a bunkhouse. There was a machinery shed, a store, stables and horse yards, a first-aid station and a schoolhouse. Further on was the helicopter pad and the runway.

She had several games of golf on the very natural nine-hole course with its sand greens. It was quite a test and it was not uncommon to dodge the odd wallaby or emu with chicks in tow. Or to be deafened by the flock of raucous corellas, very similar to cockatoos but without the yellow crest, birds that often blanketed the scrubby trees beside the fairways in creamy white.

She hadn't played with Finn. He might have abandoned his stick, and seemed to be coping pretty well, she had to concede, although he still limped occasionally, but he was also being cautious with his new-won freedom.

And she spent three mornings a week at the local hospital in physiotherapy clinics, and was enjoying that very much. Not only that, she'd become a favourite with the station kids, in the first place because of her willingness to run around and referee their football games, and then, of course, because of the incident over the pianola.

She'd asked permission, and received it, to play the pianola—it was hard on your legs at first as you pumped the pedals, but some of the timeless old songs it played fascinated her, and she sang along in her low husky voice. She also sometimes played it as a piano, she'd studied music for years as a child.

Once, as she was pumping away and singing along, the hairs on the back of her neck seemed to tell her she was not alone. She stopped abruptly and swung round on the stool to find Finn propped against a wall and watching her.

'Am I making too much noise?' she asked ruefully.

He shook his head. 'You sing well.'

'I'm a shameless singer in the shower,' she confessed. She got up, slid open the doors on the front of the pianola to remove the music roll, and put it carefully back in its box.

'You don't have to stop on my account. It's probably doing it good to be played,' he said.

'I know who would love it,' she said without thinking. 'The station kids.'

Finn looked around the gallery and looked faintly alarmed.

'Oh, I would never bring them in here. By the way, it needs tuning.' She closed the cover.

He straightened. 'I suppose if they were supervised and not allowed to touch anything—'

'No,' she interrupted with a grin. 'Too much responsibility for me to take on.'

He watched her for a moment, then shrugged and walked away, leaving her feeling curiously repulsed.

However, two days later, a piano tuner arrived from Toowoomba and the pianola disappeared from the gallery and reappeared in a solid storeroom attached to the schoolhouse that had been cleaned up and made comfortable. It was eventually replaced in the gallery by a brand-new conventional piano delivered by road.

Finally, the key to the storeroom was presented to Sienna.

'But…but…all this and I won't be here for that long,' she protested.

'Someone will take your place,' Finn said, and that was all he said.

She looked down at the key in her palm, and couldn't decide if she was annoyed or pleased with his arbitrary decision to bring some music into the lives of the children who lived on Waterford. Then she realized it was the arbitrary nature of it, which just about summed Finn McLeod up in a nutshell anyway, that got to her.

She closed her eyes as this thought struck her, and decided it was unworthy of her, in this instance.

And she'd been right, the kids adored the pianola and she soon had them singing along with gusto with her as she pumped energetically. "Roll Out The Barrel" was one of their favourites—they almost lifted the roof with it.

But it was after her refereeing a game that she had a memorable encounter with Finn…

She came back to the homestead scarlet in the face and covered in dust. She collapsed in a veranda chair to catch her breath before taking a much-needed shower, then leapt to her feet as a snake slithered across the veranda. After her first movement, she didn't scream, she didn't panic, she stood quite still as she watched it disappear over the edge of the veranda into the shrubbery.

Then she took a very deep shuddery breath and said aloud and with great feeling, 'Yuck, I *hate* snakes!'

'Then you gave a pretty good imitation of not particularly minding them,' an amused voice said. She turned to see Finn had come round a corner of the veranda behind her.

She shrugged. 'That's training, that's all, part of a first-aid course I did. If I'm any judge it was a young carpet snake, not usually aggressive and much more interested in getting away.'

'Spot on,' he agreed, coming to stand beside her, 'but the reality of them can be a whole different matter for many people.'

She looked up at him somewhat darkly. 'I suppose you *like* them. I suppose you were expecting an "all-luxury, city girl" type of response from me?'

He raised his eyebrows. 'That obviously still rankles, but no.' He looked her over, taking in her sweat-streaked dirty face, her dusty shorts and sand shoes, the strands of hair plastered to her neck.

In contrast he looked clean and cool in cargo shorts and a checked shirt, tall and well made and altogether more good-looking than was good for any one man, she thought rebelliously.

He frowned. 'No,' he repeated. 'In fact I have to ask myself this—why did you make such a fuss about coming out here? You couldn't have fitted in better.'

Sienna opened her mouth, closed it and gritted her teeth for a moment. Then she said precisely, 'What I make a fuss about is my affair, Finn McLeod, not yours.' And she turned to stride away from him.

'Incidentally,' he said, 'I don't like snakes at all.'

But she was too annoyed to acknowledge this as a peace overture so she kept on walking.

It not only annoyed her, that exchange, however, in the context that she felt damned because she *had* fitted in—was there any pleasing the man?—it had bothered her.

Because she could see Finn visibly relaxing as he was able to get out and about on the cattle run, driven by Dave or in the station helicopter—relaxing, except, that was, with her...

It started to trouble her obscurely, then more openly. She suddenly realized she missed that camaraderie, that it had meant more to her than she'd understood at the time.

But now, when they worked together in the newly-fitted gym, she could feel the restraint in him as she helped him to exercise his leg. She even got the feeling her light-hearted patter irritated him, so she gradually fell silent.

Then it occurred to her that he didn't particularly like

the feel of her hands on his powerful, streamlined body, which made no sense at all because she'd been handling him in a medically related way for weeks, guiding his movements et cetera.

But whatever his problems were and whether her own grew out of that blank wall she sensed she was dealing with in him, she had to admit she was starting to feel curiously bruised herself.

What was she doing wrong? She'd changed nothing in her approach that she could see.

It was the effect of that "bruised" feeling that stunned her. She suddenly found herself thinking of Finn McLeod more as an individual than a patient and then, to her amazement, and concern, as a man. But in a much more serious way than being made to feel a bit "tingly", although these thoughts also came in little flashes.

She'd watched him once holding a conference with the mustering team. He'd worn jeans and a khaki bush shirt, boots and a stockman's hat. He'd looked tall and lean and fit.

He'd looked very much a figure of authority as he'd stood in the shade of a peppercorn tree on the beaten earth square in front of the stockmen's bunkhouse, but also very human as he'd rested his hand on the head of one of the cattle dogs that had been grinning up at him adoringly.

He'd looked—her heart had started to beat rapidly as she'd realized it—incredibly attractive in the way that made you wonder what it would be like to go to bed with Finn McLeod.

She'd slipped away from the conference rather abruptly, and taken stern issue with herself. Where had her "fireproof" status regarding men gone? Was she actually coming out of the vacuum she'd found herself in after James's defection? But with a patient!

Of course, he was more than that now. She'd become part of his lifestyle and that could account for a heightened awareness of him but—it still wasn't on, she told herself. Remember Angelo's, she admonished herself, and Eastwood. Yes, Waterford might be much more relaxed and informal, but it was only a part of Finn's life. The rest of it came with private jets, exclusive restaurants, designer-clothed women who spent more on their wardrobes and in their beauty salons than she could probably imagine…

Still, there was Alice McLeod, she reminded herself, who'd obviously lived a very useful life but…

A big but, she thought with an inward grimace. Apart from anything else, what sane girl would take on the memories of Holly Pearson?

All the same, she'd had another embarrassing lapse. They'd all been in the games room one evening, she'd been playing chess with Walt, and beating him, the others had been playing billiards, even Finn.

She'd found her gaze drawn to him frequently while Walt had made heavy weather of pondering his next move.

In an open-necked white shirt and fawn moleskins with his thick dark hair sometimes falling in his eyes as he'd lined up a shot, Finn had been magnetic in a way that had made the pulse at the base of her throat beat erratically.

But it hadn't been only his stream-lined body that she'd found magnetic, it had been his hands as he'd balanced the cue, it had been the flash of humour and the quip he'd tossed off that had made everyone laugh when he'd pocketed the ball, it had been just about everything about him, she'd thought dazedly.

So dazedly, she'd lost concentration and had to suffer a humiliating checkmate from Walt as she'd wondered why Finn could be like that with everyone but herself.

The next morning brought Declan into their midst with a party of five friends he intended to fly on to Carnarvon Gorge for a camping weekend.

He arrived without warning, apart from buzzing the homestead and calling up on his VHF radio at the same time, in his own plane.

For the first time, Sienna heard Walt swear audibly, but from that moment on he reacted like a smooth but high-powered dynamo.

She happened to be at the refectory table having a cup of morning tea—she'd been out for a ride—when Walt took the VHF call. He hung up the mike, swore, and immediately called Finn on the in-house phone. 'Six people altogether, three couples, they plan to stay one night, they're all golfers so I thought of a golf comp this afternoon, a big dinner tonight and maybe they'd like to dance. Will I put them in the Green House or move Dave and Miss Torrance—?'

He stopped talking and nodded several times, then put the phone down. 'You can stay where you are, Miss Torrance,' he said, and called for the cook and the housekeeper, who arrived on the double, looking excited. They'd obviously recognized the buzzing plane and knew what it usually meant: some excitement in their lives, Sienna judged.

When they left after menus for lunch and dinner had been discussed and agreed upon and the Green House had been ordered to be brought up to scratch swiftly—one of the orders there had caused Sienna to smile ruefully: Check for snakes and spiders, it hasn't been used for a while and city girls don't like 'em—she said to Walt, 'I do believe you're worth your weight in gold, Mr Butler! Is there anything I could do, though?'

'Uh—yes. Would you mind organizing a golf competition for me, Miss Torrance? Check with our mob who'd like to be in it, make sure there are enough clubs, score cards, tees and balls.'

'I can tell you there aren't enough clubs unless we restrict it to a driver, an iron, and a putter.'

'That'll do. Thank you!' He got up, and as he left Finn strolled in.

Sienna had just poured herself a second cup of tea and she sipped it as she waited for him to make the first move—that was how unsure she was of him these days, she reflected.

He sat down opposite her and poured his own tea. 'You're aware that we're about to be inundated?' he queried.

'I am. I've also been put in charge of the golf this afternoon.' She paused. Because Finn hadn't as yet added golf to his accomplishments, although he had started to drive a car, she discovered herself feeling suddenly awkward. 'It wasn't my idea.'

'I know. Anything that keeps them occupied is a good idea, however.'

'What will you do?' She regretted the question no sooner than it left her lips—if anything was calculated to make him feel his deficiencies, that might be it.

'What do you suggest?' It was said evenly, but she could see the tinge of irony in his expression. 'Should I take up crocheting coat-hanger covers?'

'Finn,' she bit her lip, 'no, of course not. I didn't mean—look, you've achieved *so* much and it's only a matter of time before you'll be playing golf again so—'

'Don't.' He dragged a hand through his dark hair. 'Don't bloody patronize me, Sienna,' he said through his teeth. 'Keep your bright patient talk for patients who need it. I don't.'

He got up, picked up his cup and saucer and walked out.

She stared after him, horrified and disbelieving. She half rose to follow him and take issue with him, but Declan and his party chose that moment to arrive.

At six o'clock that evening, Sienna thankfully closed herself into her suite and went immediately to take a shower.

As the tank water streamed down her hair and body, she reviewed the afternoon. The golf competition had been fun. Declan's friends were all about the same age as he was, obviously a swinging set from their conversation that had frequent references to the races, so-and-so's party, golf courses around the world they'd played on, yachts they'd crewed on, et cetera. But the women were friendly and the men enthusiastic, not only about Waterford, but their up-coming camping expedition.

Somewhat to her embarrassment, Sienna and her partner, one of Finn's pilots, had won the golf competition, but no one seemed to mind.

More importantly perhaps, she didn't think anyone had divined her true state of mind—serious perturbation, in other words.

Finn had greeted the golfing party back at the homestead and, just as he'd been at lunch and earlier, you wouldn't have known his mood was anything but congenial.

But how could it be?

She switched off the taps, dried herself, slipped on her robe and sat down to blow dry her hair as she asked herself a question.

How could she have got so seriously off-base with Finn McLeod?

Was it a psychological problem he was battling? she wondered. Did he believe he was never going to get to full, free mobility? Never get to play golf again, perhaps? But she did, so…Should she ring Peter Bannister? she wondered. Maybe she did need another opinion or another approach?

Why was she so upset, though?

She switched the dryer off and watched her hair subside in a shiny, smooth fall.

Well, she had every reason to be upset. She wasn't the one who'd insisted she come to Waterford. All the same, she couldn't help feeling she'd failed somewhere along the line.

Not only that, she had to concede, apart from the therapeutic side of things, she was beginning to hate being in discord with Finn. She was beginning to have all sorts of crazy thoughts about him, which definitely didn't make sense in this new context between them.

Time to take herself off Finn McLeod's case? she asked herself. She straightened her spine. Yes, and the sooner the better, but maybe not tonight.

Her shoulders slumped as she thought of getting through a "big" dinner, then dancing. Dancing! Something else Finn McLeod couldn't do yet—would it put him in an even worse mood?

She clicked her tongue rather savagely, and got up to dress.

She was flicking through her slender wardrobe when she decided she would avoid the dancing. She'd slip away quietly and come to bed. In which case she need not worry too much about what to wear, and she chose slim violet linen trousers and a carnation-pink silk blouse.

'And I'd like to propose a toast to Sienna!' Declan McLeod said. 'Not only a damn good golfer, but a sight for sore eyes and a miracle worker, apparently.'

Sienna hid a grimace as everyone raised their glasses to her and chorused her name.

No refectory table for this dinner—they were in the dining room where several generations of McLeods looked down at them from the walls, where the mahogany chairs had sapphire-blue velvet upholstered seats that matched the curtains, and an exquisite ornate

antique silver punch bowl filled with flowers held pride
of place in the centre of the table.

It had been a magnificent meal. Smoked salmon with
capers followed by roast, crackling-crisp-to-perfection
pork and apple sauce with roast potatoes and pumpkin
and a cauliflower au gratin dish. Dessert had been a
brandy pudding.

Declan's party was at the gently rollicking stage, as
was Declan himself, she judged, hence the several toasts
he'd proposed. Definitely time for coffee, then some
gentle exercise, she decided, and discovered Walt was
of the same mind.

'Coffee will be served in the gallery,' he announced.

Sienna placed her napkin on the table and stood up.
'Thank you, Walt. Let's go, shall we?' she said at large,
and suddenly found herself looking into Finn's eyes.

He'd played his part well during the meal. Not over-
talkative, but amusing at times and informative at
others. But what she saw in his eyes was something
else. A sort of frowning critical assessment aimed
squarely at her.

What have I done now? she wondered with a pang,
followed by the thought that the sooner she got away
from this gathering, the better; come to that, the sooner
she got away from Waterford, the better.

It proved harder to get away from the gathering than
she'd anticipated.

It was Finn, to her horror, who asked her to play the
new piano while they recovered from the meal and had
their coffee.

It was Declan who enthusiastically seconded the request.

'By—golly gosh!' he said. 'Don't tell me you're artistic too, Sienna? No wonder—well, please do!'

'No wonder—what?' Sienna enquired coolly. She was beginning to feel exhausted and very much put upon.

'Nothing! Go ahead.' He opened the piano and pulled the stool out.

Sienna hesitated, then she closed the lid and pushed the stool in. 'Look,' she said with a wry smile, 'I play for my own enjoyment, that's all. That can be excruciating for others to bear so I won't put you through it. But we do have music, don't we?'

Finn, having thrown her in head first, in a manner of speaking, chose to come to her rescue. 'Sure,' he said easily, and opened the doors of the cabinet that housed the sound system. 'We do,' he added with a curious sort of significance and an odd little glance at her.

Half an hour later Sienna did make her escape, but instead of going to bed—she had the feeling sleep wasn't going to come easily—she decided to stroll through the garden for a bit.

She fetched a light jumper. It cooled down quite a bit after dark on the inland plains, but it was a wonderful place to watch the stars.

She had a favourite bench under a gum-tree but she was only half-way to it when Finn overtook her as she paused several times to breathe the fresh, chilly air and the night scents of the garden.

She stopped as he loomed up beside her. 'What now, Finn McLeod?' she said wearily as she looked up at him.

He wore a navy shirt and jeans, but his expression was entirely enigmatic.

'Nothing. I wondered where you were going, that's all.'

'Nowhere,' she said flatly. 'Just a stroll, then bed, or—do I need your permission for that?'

'Not at all. I gather you're annoyed with me?'

'Finn,' she began, then wondered *where* to begin—and changed tack entirely. 'I have a headache, that's all.'

It was true enough, she realized, although hardly "all".

His lips twisted into a chiselled smile full of irony. 'How convenient,' he murmured.

She gazed at him uncomprehendingly. 'There's nothing convenient about it,' she denied, then her eyes changed. 'Unless you imagine I manufactured it? But whatever for?'

He shrugged. 'It's become an historic excuse.'

She set her teeth. 'I didn't for one moment imagine you were about to ask me to go to bed with you.'

'No?'

She stared at him with her heart in her mouth as it suddenly occurred to her he might have divined her current state of mind, her astonishing reversal of feelings on the subject. But how had she given herself away—if she had? She had no idea. She also had no doubt it wouldn't be welcome to him...

So why was the air between them threaded with a peculiar tension, with an almost hypnotic awareness as the lively sounds of Declan's party swelled and ebbed on the cool night air?

It was as if her horizons had shrunk, as if the dark gardens and shining stars had been blotted out and only Finn filled her vision and her senses. As if every breath she took brought the impact of him to her more and more finely so her senses whirled a little as her pores seemed to drink him in—his tall, lean lines and powerful shoulders, those memorable features, those enigmatic blue eyes that often baffled her, his hands...

But why should he be studying her almost, she thought dazedly, intimately: the fall of her hair, the rise and fall of her breasts beneath the pink silk of her blouse? Why would he be making her aware of her figure beneath her clothes? Why would his eyes linger on the curve of her hips in a way that made her feel as if his hands were on them?

'Well,' he said at last, as if deliberately setting out to break the spell, 'maybe not, but it has other applications these days.'

It was like tumbling down to earth on a meteor for her. The hard bump of reality that sent shock waves through her. What had she been thinking? She must have imagined a reciprocal interest in him! And her face flamed with the embarrassment of it, although at least the darkness might have concealed the worst of that.

'What—' she moistened her lips '—what application would that be?'

'If you have a grievance, Sienna, don't hide behind a headache. Spit it out.'

Her eyes dilated, not only at the harshness of his voice, but the sheer unfairness of what he'd said.

She had to clear her throat to get her voice working.

Then she stopped to pinch herself metaphorically, to remind herself that, above all, this man was a patient.

'Finn,' she said with difficulty, 'it's not my place to have grievances. Your health welfare is my only concern.' And she turned and walked away surprisingly steadily.

She was not to know that he watched her, without moving, until she was out of sight, then he swore audibly.

CHAPTER FOUR

THEY farewelled Declan's rather hung-over party the next morning.

It struck Sienna as she watched them pile into the vehicle that was taking them to the landing strip that there was a strange attitude towards Declan McLeod amongst the staff—and Finn, for that matter. One of— forbearance? she pondered. But if so, why? He would have had all the advantages Finn had had despite a different mother. Was it because he so obviously didn't measure up to Finn?

She shook her head and went to work.

On the long drive into Augathella she debated, not Declan, but her own position. And she decided she rather desperately needed to talk to Peter Bannister, not so much for guidance, but because she'd be leaving Waterford as soon as possible.

She arrived ten minutes early and took the time to do just that. But Peter Bannister was not available for the next three days—he was on a camping holiday up on Cape York with his family and out of mobile range.

Sienna cursed all campers, quite irrationally, before starting work.

When she got back to Waterford, almost of the mindset that she was entitled simply to leave, although how was another matter, it was to find that Finn had flown out but only on an overnight visit to Sydney.

'He'll be back tomorrow afternoon, Miss Torrance,' Walt informed her. 'He's taken Dave with him—he asked me particularly to tell you not to be concerned.' Walt paused as if to let that sink in, then he looked faintly humorous. 'He also suggested you relax. I didn't tell him that was a bit like asking the wind to sit down and twiddle its thumbs, but—' he looked at her keenly '—maybe it's not a bad idea.'

Sienna opened her mouth to reply with a question— as in, Why? Did she look frazzled?—but thought better of it. 'Thanks, Walt, I will,' she murmured, then was struck by a thought. 'So—has everyone gone? All the guys, the pilots, the secretary, the lot?'

He nodded. 'You have the place to yourself.'

'Glory be,' she murmured with heartfelt relief, and immediately took herself to her suite where she closed herself in and studied herself in the bedroom mirror.

It was no comfort to see that, not only did she look tired and strained, but she also hadn't missed the jibe behind Finn's message, a play on her last words to him the night before about his physical welfare being her only concern.

It wasn't so surprising she looked tired, though. She hadn't slept much last night after her encounter with Finn in the garden, but how mortifying that even the staff were noticing her air of strain…

At least she was on her own, though, in a relative way, and that had to help. At least she could take time to smell the roses, so to speak, before Finn came back and she told him she was leaving.

She succeeded in the first part of her plan; the second part turned out to be another matter.

For the first part, she did more than smell the roses. She indulged at her leisure in a timeless ritual to deal with stress. She raided the herb garden and spent a bit of time in the kitchen with the cook's permission and quite some curiosity.

Sienna had made friends with Mrs Walker, the masterful lady who commanded the kitchen at Waterford.

Then she bore to her suite an oatmeal face-mask, a decoction of rosemary and camomile for her hair and a muslin bag full of lavender flowers. She smoothed the mask on her face, ran water into the tub over the lavender bag, rubbed the decoction into her hair and soaked in the bath listening to Mozart from the bedroom radio.

Then she showered and, feeling refreshed, she massaged moisturizer into her skin and did her nails. Finally she curled up on her bed with a book until the dinner gong sounded.

She ate a light meal, played the piano for an hour or so and went to bed to sleep like a top.

Curiously, as had his tormenting presence been taken from her, so had her troubled thoughts to do with Finn McLeod left her.

The next morning brought rain, a steady drumming

on the roof and the gurgle of the downpipes as the precious water streamed into the underground tanks.

It was such a different scenario from the harsh sunlight and the dust, she was amazed and fascinated. She donned a waterproof and boots and tramped round the garden. It obviously survived well enough on bore water, but she got the feeling that if plants could talk they'd be telling her this was sheer heaven even though they might be bowing their heads a little under the heavy drops at the moment.

It also occurred to her that rain, in these parts, was a mind-altering experience. She no longer felt stressed; she felt renewed.

It had stopped raining when Finn and the others arrived back, but she was not there to greet them.

She'd gone for a ride when the weather had cleared, enchanted by the new, clean, shiny world that was now Waterford.

'Take it easy, ma'am,' the ringer who'd saddled a horse for her had advised. 'Could be slippery out there.'

'I will,' she'd promised. 'What's his name?'

'Big Red.'

'He's well named—I'm going to need a leg up. Thanks!' she said once she was hoisted into the saddle.

'He's the only one in the stables or I could have found you a smaller horse, ma'am,' the ringer apologized, 'but they're all in the paddock. He's got a lovely temperament, though, this fella.'

'OK, Big Red, I hope you enjoy this as much as I plan to!'

She rode off with a wave and she *was* careful until a cow and its bogged calf decided matters otherwise for her about five miles from the homestead. The calf was bawling as it struggled and the cow was mooing its head off as it circled the area.

She sized up the situation and knew it was beyond her to rescue the calf, she could only go back for help. She took a hurried set of directions from the sun and a low, flat-topped hill in the vicinity and she dropped the red bandanna she wore round her neck over a prickly bush as a signpost.

But in her anxiety for the stricken calf and its desperate mother, she urged Big Red out of the easy canter they'd travelled at. After a mile or two, he stumbled and pecked, only momentarily, but enough for her to sail over his head.

She landed heavily. Fortunately quick thinking had seen her kick her feet out of the stirrups, but she was winded all the same.

The horse came back to her immediately and nudged her almost apologetically.

'It's all right,' she told him. 'I guess it was my fault. Just give me a minute.' She struggled to sit up and rubbed her face, but that was a mistake because her face was now streaked with mud as well as the rest of her.

But worse than that, once on her feet and reassured that she didn't seem to have broken anything, she just didn't have the strength to mount Big Red.

'Trouble is, you were always too big for me, mate, and now I'm as weak as a cat as well, but surely there must be something around I can stand on!'

There wasn't. No handy tree stump, no rocks, just

miles of wet Spinifex. On top of that the sun was sinking low on the horizon and it would be dark in an hour.

'Look,' she continued her one-sided conversation with the horse as she stroked his nose, 'I reckon it's a good three miles back so I'm not going to exhaust myself trying to mount you, I'm going to walk alongside you until *something* comes up I can stand on.'

Big Red harrumphed.

'Good, you approve,' she said. 'But one more thing, if we're not home by the time it gets dark, I may need you to navigate for me. All horses know their way home, don't they?'

A rather painful hour later, she was stiff and sore in all sorts of improbable places and she was still walking beside the patient horse. Darkness had just fallen. Earlier—although she wasn't sure how much, she'd broken her watch—she'd heard a plane and guessed it was Finn and party returning. She'd tensed as she'd wondered how this exploit of hers would be greeted and she'd started to talk to the horse again to take her mind off it.

'You do have a lovely temperament, Big Red,' she told him. 'Most horses would have taken off by now with thoughts of tucker on their mind if nothing else. Do you think there are dingoes out here?' She shivered suddenly as she looked around and thought of the trapped calf.

But Big Red stopped suddenly and whickered.

A moment later the glow of headlights—it had to be that—lit the horizon.

'I do believe we're about to be rescued! Oh, dear!' She looked down at herself. 'I feel a right idiot.'

* * *

It was Finn and a station hand who found her.

'Sienna,' Finn said ominously as he descended from the Land Rover, 'what the hell have you been doing?'

'I fell off my horse, all my fault, he's actually a lovely horse but I was in a hurry to get help to save a bogged calf and then I couldn't get back on, he's a bit too big for me. Oh, thank heavens you've come! We can go back and get the calf out.'

'We'll do no such thing. I'll drive you home and Steve here will ride the horse,' Finn said harshly. 'Have you hurt—?'

But Sienna burst into tears. The station hand, Steve, looked away in embarrassment and Finn raked a hand through his hair.

'Sienna, it's dark,' he growled. 'We could drive around for hours and not find it.'

'No! I've been watching the stars, I know the direction to take, just follow the evening star and, anyway, you can hear them from quite a way away. Besides,' she sobbed, 'you've got ropes, headlights and—and in a vehicle it won't take any time at all!'

'You're in no fit state to be driving around, Sienna!'

'Finn,' she said through her teeth, 'I would *know* if I'd broken anything or done any serious damage. Do you think I could have walked as far as I have otherwise?'

'It could have died already, while you were walking as far as you have.'

'Oh, don't make me feel worse!' she wept, then stamped her foot. 'I'll never forgive you if you don't do this, Finn McLeod!' She glared at him with her hands on her hips, completely unconscious of her muddy disarray.

'Uh—just a thought, boss,' Steve intervened. 'It could be the five mile soak. That's in the right direction, if she's got her directions right.'

'If,' Finn repeated sceptically, then, 'OK. You ride, we'll drive, but don't blame me if it's a long evening.'

Sienna waited until they were in the vehicle out of earshot of Steve before she said in low, trembling tones, 'I hate you.'

'Yes, well—' he cast her an amused glance before he drove off '—perhaps you should think twice before you ride around in muddy conditions on a horse that's too big for you.'

That effectively silenced Sienna as they bumped over the rough country. That and the fact that he activated the GPS on the dashboard and got from it a heading for the five mile soak.

Please don't let me be wrong, she prayed. For more reasons than one.

She wasn't wrong, she was the one who saw her bandanna in the headlights, still hanging on the bush as they came to the five mile soak, but the calf wasn't dead. It wasn't there.

There was no sign of it or its mother, although there was plenty of evidence of hoof prints around the churned-up mud soak that told their own tale.

'Oh, thank heavens!' Sienna breathed. 'It must have freed itself. You can take me home now.'

The silence that greeted this pronouncement was loaded.

* * *

They walked up the homestead front steps side by side.

They'd not exchanged a word on the drive back from the soak, but Sienna said as she advanced up the stairs with a hand to her back, 'What a pity you couldn't have seen me last night, Mr McLeod! I was much more presentable.' She bent to take off her boots and winced.

'What's that supposed to mean?'

'Nothing.' She rose painfully. 'Just came to mind as the height of irony. All right, I need a bath, so if you wouldn't mind delaying your lecture until then I'd appreciate it.'

'Sienna, don't be ridiculous,' he said shortly. 'I was worried, we were all worried about you.'

'Yes, we were!' Mrs Walker agreed as she bustled onto the veranda. 'But here you are, safe and sound, so all's well that ends well and you just come with me!' She put her arm around Sienna and started to lead her inside. She paused at the doorstep and said to Finn over her shoulder, 'Pity you didn't see her last night, boss!'

A hot bath helped enormously even without the soothing benefit of lavender flowers, and Mrs Walker insisted she put on a nightgown and dressing gown and told her she would be serving her dinner on a tray-table in her sitting room.

But it was Finn who brought her dinner, and sat down opposite her.

Sienna glanced warily at him, then lifted the lid on an individual dish of beef, red wine and mushroom casserole that smelled divine.

'Nothing to say, Sienna?' he murmured.

'I was waiting for you to fire the first salvo.'

He grimaced. 'Why does everyone seem to feel I should have seen you last night?'

Their gazes clashed, his faintly quizzical, hers deeply embarrassed.

'Not everyone,' she said stiffly. 'Only one person, in fact.'

'Two if you count yourself.'

Her shoulders slumped. She'd picked up her knife and fork, but put them down again in some frustration for several reasons. It was almost impossible not to be acutely aware of Finn McLeod these days, even after you'd fallen off a horse, tramped for miles and so on.

You still weren't too weary and sore to appreciate the set of his shoulders beneath a grey T-shirt or his lean, compact waist disappearing into his jeans. The springy darkness of his hair was an invitation to run your fingers through it. That memorable face with its decisive mouth, that sometimes rapier-like dense blue gaze—it all got to you no matter what.

On top of this to have to recount how you'd behaved in an essentially feminine and probably trivial way was especially galling, but she had no doubt he would get it out of her somehow.

'People were telling me I ought to relax, people were accusing me of cherishing grievances and not to be concerned—' she shot him a telling little glance '—so I did something about it.'

'What would have been so riveting about that?'

'There are ways of relaxing, if you're a girl, that make you look better and therefore feel better. I gave myself a face-pack—' she gestured widely '—the whole works, if you must know.'

He raised an eyebrow. 'It must have been pretty effective.'

Her eyebrows shot up.

'Uh—allow me to amend that,' he said ruefully. 'You must have looked a lot more relaxed. You always look very well groomed, unless you've been refereeing mad football games and falling off your horse.'

Sienna drew a deep breath. 'I'm quite sure only Mrs Walker noticed and only because she helped with the herbs and everything else.' A tinge of humour lit her eyes this time. 'But from a therapeutic point of view, it was effective. It was also rather a waste of time.' She looked at her nails, fingered a scratch on her cheek and patted the pad of one finger to a bruise beginning to show on her jaw line.

'Any more of those?' he asked.

'A few,' she admitted, and picked up her knife and fork again. 'Well, your turn.'

'We'll fly you into Augathella by helicopter for some checks tomorrow.'

'Oh! You don't need to do that. I'm sure—'

'Don't argue, Sienna. Eat your dinner.'

He waited while she did so in a rather perplexed silence, then he said, 'What were you expecting?'

Sienna pushed the dish away and took a sip of water. 'To be told I'd been stupid again, I suppose.' She shrugged.

'I've never seen you do anything blatantly stupid. Accidents do happen.'

She sighed. 'I could have been more careful. It was

just so lovely to be out there in the first place; then I was worried about the calf.'

He smiled unexpectedly. 'I know what you mean—plus, we needed that rain. And there could be more on the way. Incidentally, I went to see a specialist while I was in Sydney.'

She looked across at him alertly. 'And?' she breathed.

'He was of the opinion I could discontinue the physio-therapy. He said that with plenty of walking I would soon be—playing golf and tripping the light fantastic.'

'That's wonderful news, Finn. I told you!' Her eyes shone with enthusiasm.

'So you did.' He watched her for a moment. 'So I'm formally ending my association with you, Sienna, and I've written to Peter. He's out beyond the black stump somewhere.'

'I know that,' she said ruefully.

He paused and narrowed his eyes. 'Have you been trying to get in touch with him?'

She hesitated. 'Yes.'

'What for?'

To tell him or not to tell him? But why go into that now? She was off the hook…

'I like to keep in touch with him. So—so I'll be going home?'

He shook his head decisively. 'Not immediately. You deserve a while to recover. Anyway, the plane will be away for a few days on a maintenance call.'

She stared at him. 'You've been—nicer about this than, well, you have,' she said quietly. 'I'm sorry I got a bit carried away.'

He studied her damp hair and the deep iris-blue of her robe, and the bruise on her jaw that was turning blue itself. Then his lips twisted. 'I quite understand.' He stood up and relieved her of the tray. 'Try and get a good sleep.'

But he paused and their gazes locked again.

Sienna took an unexpected breath and let it out carefully. What was in those blue eyes that was so riveting, so—compelling? So that she felt as if she were standing on the edge of a chasm with all her senses too finely tuned and under siege?

So that, when he turned away at last and left the room, she felt unaccountably let down?

It was not the most comfortable night, but there was an element to it that had nothing to do with her bruises.

Why wasn't she happier about being off the hook with Finn McLeod?

Why was she disconcerted, bothered and bewildered? Because he'd been the one to do it rather than her?

Surely not! So did she still feel a sense of failure with him as a patient? But that didn't make sense either because she'd succeeded with him, in fact. But he had been the one to terminate their professional relationship before she would have done so herself. Still…

A sense of failure with him as a man, then?

It was a question she discovered she didn't want to explore too deeply—why? Did it have the distinct aura of a Pandora's box?

Finn was as good as his word.

Sienna was flown to the hospital the next day and

checked over thoroughly despite her protests that there was no need.

'All in one piece, told you,' she informed him when he was on the helipad to greet her on her return. But it was with a hand to her back that she'd descended, somewhat painfully, from the chopper.

He studied her wordlessly for a long moment, until she felt a tinge of embarrassment.

'I do appreciate the thought, though,' she added a little stiffly.

'I'm glad there's something you appreciate about me,' he replied.

Sienna stared up into his eyes and was visited by an extraordinary urge to tell him that what she would most appreciate from him was to be somewhere quiet and comfortable with him, but more…To be cradled in his arms, her sore body soothed. Perhaps to be kissed gently and fussed over.

She closed her eyes as the images filled her mind and she breathed deeply as her breasts rose and fell.

'Sienna?'

Her lashes flew up and a tide of heat rushed into her cheeks.

'What?' he queried, eyeing her narrowly: her eyes, the curve of her mouth, the movement of her body beneath her blameless white cotton shirt.

'N-nothing,' she stammered, turning away hurriedly. 'I—I have been told to rest for a couple of days so I'll do—just that.'

'I'll drive you to the house.'

'Oh!' She'd have given anything to be able to decline the offer, but that would only look foolish. 'Thanks.'

They said nothing on the short journey to the house, but it was another painful little interlude for Sienna.

She couldn't block the impact of so many little things about Finn from her consciousness. His wrists of all things affected her strangely, narrow but strong and sprinkled with dark hairs.

But his aura was another matter. He looked rather forbidding, the couple of times she stole a glance at him after sternly but unsuccessfully admonishing herself to keep her eyes to herself. As if he was thinking his own thoughts that had no connection to her—as if she might not even be there!

He also delivered her to the front steps and drove off immediately.

Sienna took herself to her bedroom feeling downcast and depressed. But one thing was for sure, she decided, she needed to get away. She was becoming far too physically impressionable—she stopped as she thought it and shivered—towards a man who was exhibiting all the signs of not even liking her.

Two days later, the plane was still away on maintenance and she was no further forward in her quest to leave Waterford, and Dave approached her.

He and the "guys", other than Finn, had decided to drive into town for the annual rodeo. They planned to be home about nine o'clock. Therefore, he had a request. If Sienna wasn't particularly into rodeos, would she mind standing in for him because he didn't like to leave Finn without someone who knew what they were doing just in case he fell over or something like that?

Sienna hesitated but only briefly. She liked Dave and he'd been easy to work with. But what Dave requested next gave her food for thought.

He asked her not to let Finn know she was standing in for him.

'I know he's got the go-ahead from the specialist so I don't want him to feel he needs a baby-sitter. He gets a bit—funny about that, has for a while now,' Dave said, striving for delicacy. 'He's also moved me out to the annexe—closer to the other guys, he said. True, but I think he wants real independence now.'

'I quite understand, don't worry,' she replied, but she thought privately, if Finn was touchy with Dave too, maybe the problem hadn't been with herself, *per se*, but with everyone keeping an eye on him?

She spent the afternoon quietly, working on her case notes, and dinner, as usual, was a communal affair with the household staff who hadn't gone to the rodeo.

But there was no sign of Finn after dinner and she guessed he was closeted in the study. All the same, rather than retiring to her sitting room with her book, she curled up in an armchair with it in the games room.

He came in an hour later and seemed surprised to see her.

'I thought you'd gone to bed, Sienna, it's so quiet.'

She watched him for a moment as he stood beside the billiard table, as if he was in two minds about something.

'No, but it is very nice and peaceful, isn't it?'

He hesitated. 'Yes. Why didn't you go to the rodeo? It's quite an event.'

Sienna closed her book and put it on a side table. 'Just didn't feel like it.' She shrugged.

'No?' He frowned. 'I would have thought—' He paused. 'Or—you wouldn't be standing in for Dave, by any chance?'

Sienna grimaced inwardly—how to get out of that one?

'You are,' he said flatly, 'but if you think I need a nursemaid, particularly you, you're mistaken.'

Sienna sprang up with her chin raised haughtily, all set to tell him that was fine with her but she came to grief. She'd slipped her sandals off when she'd curled up in the chair and she tripped over them.

Finn moved swiftly to save her and she ended up in his arms.

'And this,' he said barely audibly, 'is why I don't need you as a nursemaid.' He gathered her closer and bent his head to kiss her.

She froze beneath his wandering hands and lips. She was wearing hipster jeans with an aquamarine singlet top that exposed her slim midriff. He took full advantage of the gap to almost circle her waist with his hands at the same time as he kissed the hollows at the base of her throat, then he pushed aside a singlet strap and her bra strap to expose the creamy top of her breast.

She gasped as his long fingers explored further and found her nipple, and all sorts of sensations started to zing through her body; lovely, sensuous waves of feeling that rocked her even closer to him and left her powerless to resist when he transferred his mouth to hers and started to kiss her deeply.

Nothing, she thought, had prepared her for the reality of being kissed and caressed by Finn McLeod. None of those tingly feelings had come remotely close to the sheer heaven of his tall body against hers, all that clever dynamism, that banked-down masculinity no longer banked but focused solely on her and bringing her pure pleasure.

Nothing, come to that, had prepared her for the torrent of feeling for him that he unleashed in her.

So that she moved invitingly against him and submitted to his kiss willingly, even brought her hands up to cup his face then run her fingers through his hair as the heat of their bodies grew to fever pitch and she couldn't doubt his desire for her—she had no hope of hiding her own, it was too late for that.

They separated breathlessly at last, and he clasped his hands loosely around her waist. 'Does it make sense now?' he queried.

Sienna was transfixed. She heard a dog bark outside, silencing the cicada chorus briefly. She closed her eyes and when she opened them everything was as before, the same dark green walls, the same billiard table, the same chintz armchairs.

What did I expect? she wondered. That I dreamt it?

'No, you're not dreaming,' he said with a faint smile brought on by her displaced look around the room.

Sienna had her hands on his shoulders and she clenched them on the stuff of his shirt as she drifted back to earth, and reality.

'But you've been so—I didn't think you *liked* me, let alone—anything else.' Her eyes were bemused.

He smiled a little wryly and she caught her breath because just to be smiled at made her feel weak at the knees.

'It's been the opposite,' he said. 'I didn't want to—leap in where angels fear to tread,' he said with some irony, 'so soon after we ended our—professional relationship, I guess. I'm sorry if it's made me a little difficult.'

'Difficult?' she whispered because her voice didn't seem to be working properly. 'Yes, you have been difficult. You've made me feel—awful. And it just didn't make sense after telling me you needed me to be here putting my heart and soul into your rehabilitation.'

'But that's the point, isn't it? I'm sure it would have gone against the grain of your ethics if I'd made love to you while you were working with me.'

'Yes!' She said it intensely, then subsided. 'But I didn't know—I mean—' She broke off and gazed at him with sheer confusion in her eyes.

'Besides which, only a couple of days ago you did give me to understand that my health was your only concern.' He looked at her quizzically. 'Was that true?'

Sienna bit her lip.

'Whereas I've been dying to take you in my arms for quite some time now, Sienna,' he went on with some irony.

'That's—that could be patient attachment!' But as she said it, she knew she was grasping at straws.

'No, it's not,' he denied. 'At least credit me with

some sense. Being your patient has gradually become a form of torture.'

Sienna subsided again rather like a sail losing the breeze. She could only stare at him incredulously.

'Keeping my hands off you has been the same,' he added quietly. 'And *your* hands on me were even harder to bear if anything.'

'So I didn't imagine…' She trailed off.

He looked a question at her.

'I—' She cleared her throat. 'Sometimes when you looked at me I wondered, but I couldn't believe it.'

He grimaced. 'Believe it. How about you?'

Sienna shook her head, but mainly to clear it. 'Finn,' she said hoarsely, 'we don't really know each other.'

'Sienna, we've been in close physical contact for several months now, very close. Surely you can put aside your professionalism and make a personal judgement?' His blue gaze was slightly scathing. 'Don't you like me? Do I make your skin crawl? Do you find me deranged or a dead bore?'

Her breasts heaved beneath the cotton knit of her singlet as she tried to order her thoughts. 'No, obviously none of those,' she said with her own irony.

He laughed softly and kissed her forehead, then her mouth, before putting her away from him with a rueful look. 'Perhaps we should talk before we get carried away again?' he suggested.

Sienna felt the heat rush into her cheeks, all over her body, in fact. 'Yes, a good idea…' She tried to say it decisively, but her composure was sorely tried. It was as if, she thought, she were breathing rare, purified air, as if she were on a high such as she'd never known and it was all to do with Finn McLeod and the feel of his body on hers, his mouth on hers, but…

Yes, but, she thought shakily, where does it lead?

For the moment, he led her to a settee, then he disappeared for a time and reappeared with two brandies.

'Thank you,' she said with real gratitude as she took the balloon glass from him.

'Cheers,' he murmured, and took her free hand as he sat down beside her. 'How do you feel?'

'A bit like a hummingbird—all of a flutter,' she answered with a rueful look.

'That's nice.'

'Maybe. Finn—' She sobered.

'If there is anything you hold against me, you can tell me,' he said with a lurking smile.

'Well, you're a bit too used to getting your own way, but this—' She stopped helplessly. 'This, though…I'm flummoxed,' she said honestly.

'I could always try to reform—about getting my own way,' he offered with a wicked little glint in his eyes.

'And pigs might fly,' she retorted. 'Uh—' She turned to him urgently. 'Uh—you see, my real problem is I'm terrified of making another mistake, I am bitter and—confused, I guess. But one thing's for sure, I don't want to get onto that terrible emotional roller coaster again.'

'Being betrayed by your own sister had to add considerably to that.'

She sat back.

He narrowed his eyes thoughtfully. 'All the same, this is the here and now, Sienna. Things change. For me too.'

She moistened her lips. 'I don't know what to say. It's—' She broke off and stiffened at the sound of a motor outside, then looked at her watch. 'They're home early, the guys!'

Finn swore softly. 'We could relocate to my—'

'No,' she broke in swiftly. 'No, Finn. I would feel— I would feel funny about that. Honestly! I know it sounds—silly maybe, but all the same.'

'Running scared, Sienna?' he queried. 'There's no reason to be embarrassed. I'm not going to leap on you in front of them.' His lips twisted. 'Although, they may even have a fair idea of what's going on, anyway.'

A look of horror touched her grey eyes. 'How? Why?'

He shrugged. 'I have no doubt Mrs Walker has paired us if nothing else. I wouldn't be surprised if Walt has divined the true state of affairs. Staff—' he grimaced '—usually do before anyone else does. But for that matter I wouldn't be surprised if Declan is alerted to it.'

Sienna blinked frenziedly and suddenly remembered something Declan had said then refused to explain when he'd discovered she played the piano. Something that she could now interpret as—approval? Or maybe understanding of why she should be suitable for Finn and Waterford…

'Oh!' She thrust her glass of brandy into Finn's hand. 'And you think all that isn't embarrassing? How like a man!' she marvelled. 'But I have to tell you I like to be much more private about things so I'm going to bed. I'll—I'll talk to you tomorrow, Finn.'

He stood up looking half amused, half annoyed. 'Sienna—'

'On second thoughts, I'll have that back!' She took her glass of brandy from him and fled with it as fast as she could without spilling any.

When she got to the safety of the bedroom, she locked the door and took the brandy over to the dressing table for some strange reason that she soon identified as needing to see herself. Did she look the same? Did it show how much she'd enjoyed kissing Finn?

What it showed her was disordered hair, a red, ripe mouth and dazed eyes.

She reached for her brush and stroked her hair with it until it was smooth and shiny. And, despite feeling like a sixteen-year-old who'd been kissed for the first time and correspondingly foolish, she stayed at the dressing table to look steadily into her own eyes. Because there was so much to think about…

Her experience with James Haig had left her hurt and bitter, but there was more to it than she'd ever told anyone; there was a special kind of humiliation.

It had been not exactly a whirlwind romance with James. A few months of falling more and more in love with him, although—and this would plague her to the end of her life—had it been her request that they wait until they knew they were seriously committed and were sure they would marry before they slept with each other that had been her undoing?

Quite possibly, she acknowledged, and it was also the biggest source of her bitterness. Why, though, had she done it?

Because it had always weighed with her that if you

were going to give yourself to a man, it should be the right man? She had come more and more to think James was right, though, but deep in her heart she would have rather they'd married first.

Perhaps I was impossibly old-fashioned, perhaps I just don't understand men, perhaps—she paused her thoughts and shook her head—their preoccupation with getting you into bed was something I always resented?

So what does that make me? she wondered. Apart, that is, from a twenty-six-year-old who had to bargain with a virtual stranger to get him to escort her to her sister's wedding?

Something of an anomaly if nothing else, she answered herself dryly. Maybe not a very sensual person at heart. Not that I didn't enjoy James's courtship, but I could always draw the line whereas he...

He, she thought bleakly, had seen it as something of a challenge. Perhaps it had been a novel experience for him; perhaps it had added some spice.

She stared at herself in the mirror. Of course she'd also sensed James's impatience, and it had haunted her that Dakota might have had no such reservations, not that she believed her sister was promiscuous. But if an attraction had flared between Dakota and James, she could imagine Dakota giving herself generously and spontaneously, and might that not have seemed like sheer heaven to a man who had had celibacy forced on him?

She gritted her teeth and banished the images that usually arose with these thoughts.

But the fact remained, she was still a virgin. How did that fit in with this growing desire for Finn McLeod?

Did he have marriage in mind and, if so, would she want to wait?

She saw the irony in her own eyes and closed them, then took a sip of brandy to steady herself against the mental admission that she didn't think she would at all. Because she strongly suspected the torrent of feeling he'd unleashed in her for him would not be amenable to being harnessed again, but could she be *sure* she wouldn't freeze up inexplicably? Especially if he only wanted a relationship?

So, should she try to explain to Finn that she was a virgin and why?

But what about Finn himself? she wondered. It couldn't, surely, be only physical gratification he was seeking? No man with his resources, his dynamism, could lack that when and where he chose with none of the complications that had involved her. So what else was he seeking from her?

And what about the memory of Holly?

She frowned. She had read somewhere that men were more likely to look for new partners after losing one sooner than women. She'd actually seen it in her own grandfather, who'd stunned the family by falling in love in his middle seventies, with a sixty-nine-year-old widow, after losing his beloved wife of fifty years, her grandmother.

But there was a rationale for that, wasn't there?

Men were supposed to be less handy at looking after themselves than women, less able to live without love or affection. Did that sound like Finn McLeod, though?

No, she decided. On the other hand, why not?

She got up and hugged herself. The house was quiet now after the babble of conversation she'd heard when the men had come in.

It sounded as if everyone was in bed. She could even hear the call of an owl and it made her feel slightly eerie. Can you feel eerie? she wondered. Or is it lonely to think of the vast tracts of uninhabited land out there, to picture owls flitting around with the sinister beat of their wings and some poor innocent creature about to be gobbled up?

Or is it just plain lonely because you would love to be with Finn, in his bed, in his arms?

She drained the brandy and went to bed.

CHAPTER FIVE

'CARE to come for a drive, Sienna?' Finn said to her late the next afternoon.

It had been a busy day on Waterford.

A team of vets had descended on the station and all sorts of animal husbandry had been attended to: mares in foal checked, geldings performed and the ongoing tick and parasite control measures carried out on a mustered mob of cattle.

That had been fascinating, although dusty and incredibly noisy with cattle bellowing and whips cracking as the mob, one by one, had been put in a race then swum through a cattle dip.

Sienna had watched that but for the rest of the day she'd been left to her own devices.

The net result was that now she was feeling jittery because pressure seemed to be growing inside her rather like a steam engine. Because she was even beginning to doubt that the events of the previous evening had happened, or she'd misread them or something?

As in—killed them by scuttling away like a terrified rabbit?

'Yes, thank you,' she said quietly. 'I'll just get my sunglasses.'

Finn drove them silently for a couple of miles, then pulled up in the middle of nowhere.

'Let's stretch our legs.' He opened his door.

'We're—here?' she asked with a tinge of surprise.

'Why not? Out you get.'

She got out and he came round to her side of the Land Rover.

'I thought you might want to show me something.' Her voice sounded nervous to her own ears and she bit her lip.

'Oh, I do,' he drawled, looking down at her. 'I just thought, in deference to your desire for privacy, this might be a good spot.' He looked around.

Sienna followed the line of his gaze, the huge empty sky, miles of red soil and Spinifex, not even a cow in sight, and brought her gaze back to cast him a fiery little look.

'If you think that's funny, I don't!' she told him. 'I think it's very—annoying. And if you've brought me out here to kiss me, think again.'

'Strange you should say that, because I've been annoyed all day. And all because I *haven't* been able to kiss you, I've actually been a basket case.'

Sienna stared into his blue eyes, arrested in her tracks, wide-eyed and open-mouthed.

'You didn't look it!'

'I felt it. How about you?'

She opened her mouth, then closed it. 'Well—but it's still annoying to have the mickey taken out of me like this!'

'I apologize, but don't you think we both might be suffering from serious withdrawal symptoms?' His gaze rested squarely on her mouth. 'And don't you think all this annoyance floating about could be frustration instead?'

Sienna licked her lips. 'But we are cross with each other, aren't we?' she hazarded. 'I mean—' She stopped and clicked her tongue at the laughter in his eyes, then she felt herself start to melt, because he was right and an irresistible gurgle of laughter rose within her.

But she quelled it and started to speak. 'Oh, well—'

He stopped what she'd been about to say with a finger to her lips. Five minutes later, they broke apart and Sienna was trembling with desire as she leant against him to catch her breath.

She suddenly stopped as she thought back to her deliberations of the last night. 'Finn, there's something we need to discuss.' She stopped again though as static crackled in the air and a disembodied voice spoke.

'Finn, Walt here.'

Sienna blinked incredulously. Then as Finn released her, swearing under his breath, and he reached into the Land Rover, she realized it was the radio on the dash.

And the gist of Walt's message was that the shire chairman had arrived for his scheduled meeting with Finn—had he forgotten? And that he was also invited to dinner?

Finn growled a response into the microphone to the

effect that he'd be back shortly, then slammed it back onto the dashboard.

'Routed, riposted—for my sins,' he said somewhat savagely to Sienna.

She had to laugh and she did say teasingly, 'Serves you right for bringing me to the middle of a paddock to be private!'

'Yes. But—' he took her in his arms '—it must demonstrate that I have been a basket case today at least. I'd forgotten all about the bloody shire chairman.'

'Don't swear,' she murmured softly. 'It's not so serious.'

He propped himself against the Land Rover and kept her in his arms. 'It's very serious. You haven't met the guy yet. He's a walking one-man band except he doesn't sing, he talks. Dinner could go on for hours.'

'Well, I'm not going anywhere and there's always tomorrow.'

He frowned. 'What is it we need to discuss?'

She brought her hands up to cup his face. 'Not something we can talk about in haste, Finn. Tomorrow.'

He caught one of her hands and kissed her palm, then transferred his lips to hers. It was a long, searching kiss he subjected her to and an intimate exploration of her breasts that left her gasping and trembling when he finally desisted.

'So long as you're not erecting all sorts of unnecessary fences for me to fall at,' he said with his fingers hard on her waist and his eyes boring into hers.

She had to smile at the analogy, but she didn't answer—and Walt called again and put the shire chairman on, who jovially enquired what the hell Finn was doing.

* * *

The dinner did go on for hours, although Sienna excused herself fairly early on.

But she could hear the booming voice of Finn's guest even through the thick walls of the homestead until about ten o'clock. Then the house fell quiet and she fell asleep.

But around midnight she was woken by a noise she couldn't identify—a heavy thud.

She sat up again and frowned, then cast aside the bed-clothes as she wondered if Finn was still up and about and had fallen over or something. She also remembered that Dave had moved out to the annexe.

She tiptoed through the main rooms, but could find nothing amiss, yet as she hesitated outside Finn's door she heard another thud come from within.

She tapped on the door but there was no response so she opened it and took an unsteady breath at what she saw.

Moonlight was streaming in through the open curtains and Finn was writhing on the bed wearing only short pyjama bottoms. The two thuds she'd heard had come from the knocked-over bedside lamps.

'What is it?' she breathed as she rushed into the room—and the door closed behind her as a breeze blew through the house.

'What's wrong? Finn, Finn, are you—?' She stopped abruptly because the answer to her question was that he was obviously not OK.

He was taking shuddery breaths, he was covered in sweat but he felt icy cold and—to her amazement—he was asleep, or at least half asleep, as she sat down beside him and put her hand on his shoulder.

Her mind raced through the medical possibilities for his condition but she drew a blank. The only danger he was in these days *was* falling over from too much pressure on the damaged ligaments and tendons of his leg, which were all healed anyway.

It must be a nightmare, she thought as he mumbled incoherently.

'Finn,' she murmured, 'it's OK, you're home, well, you're at Waterford, in your own bed, it's OK.' And she stroked his shoulder.

His eyes flickered open and she saw dazed recognition hit him, but nothing prepared her for what happened next.

He said something that sounded like, 'Thank God,' and reached up to pull her down beside him. Then he pulled the coverlet over them and took her into his arms.

CHAPTER SIX

SIENNA opened her mouth to protest but as Finn held her she could feel his heartbeat start to slow and the shuddering start to subside. Five minutes later, his breathing deepened and although he still held her, it was in a relaxed embrace, and he fell asleep.

All the same, when she moved cautiously his arms tightened around her, and she stilled.

She wasn't uncomfortable, she decided. She had a pillow under her head and she had a well of compassion in her heart for Finn McLeod, who'd fought so bravely to regain his mobility but was still fighting other demons, demons that wouldn't let him sleep, that brought him terrible nightmares.

Of course, she could guess what they were, those demons: the accident, the loss of Holly, a life in ruins.

So, did it matter if she stayed where she was for a while? It was highly unethical—although it wasn't any longer, she recalled...

So how could she deny him some hours of sleep when she knew he needed them desperately?

She would just rest beside him peacefully for a while,

and it was amazingly peaceful, so peaceful yet so strangely companionable, she felt herself nodding off a couple of times—and finally did so.

Dawn woke her.

Pearly light tinged with apricot, coming through the windows to replace the moonlight, illuminated the room and the man beside her, watching her—Finn.

But there was more—amazingly, there was so much more. There was the warmth of his body beside hers. There was the feel of his arms around her, there was the inescapably "right" feeling of it all, and, above all, the inescapable flood of tenderness she felt for him.

Her eyes softened and she laid her hand gently on the blue shadows on his jaw. 'Better?' she whispered.

'Better,' he agreed and turned his head to kiss her palm.

She could only say later that it all led on from there, almost as if it had been preordained and she had no say, wanted no say to the contrary. When he transferred his mouth to hers, it seemed perfectly natural to kiss him back.

When he slid his hands beneath her pyjama top, she thrilled to his touch on her breasts. When he circled her waist, she found herself kissing the smooth, tanned skin of his shoulders. Then he pushed her pyjama pants down and cupped her hips, and she moved against him to the rhythm of desire that was coursing through her.

She felt like a flame dancing in the wind, quicksilver and more alive than she'd ever felt as he touched and smoothed her skin, caressed her nipples and aroused her in a way she'd never been aroused before.

And everything about him was intoxicating, his pure man aroma, the springy dark hairs on his chest, everything.

Then the moment came, and she tensed briefly and felt the surprise that coursed through him as he realized why, but his hands on her gentled immediately until the small tearing sensation receded, and once again she was thrumming with desire and ready to move on.

They moved on together, moving as one, climaxing at the same time, then holding each other hard as they slid down back to earth again.

'If only I'd known,' he said softly.

'It was fine, it was more than fine,' she reassured him, and trembled at the memory of the heights they'd reached.

'So…' he threaded his fingers through her hair '…will you marry me, Sienna?'

Her lips parted. 'Oh—I—don't know about that…' And she blushed crimson at the quizzical expression she saw in his eyes. 'I know what you must be thinking.'

'Do you?' he countered.

'Yes. It's a little strange to be in this position and in two minds but—'

'This position?' he queried 'Naked—' he drew his fingers down her flank '—sated, very lovely and showing no inclination to leave?'

Sienna grimaced and laid her cheek on his shoulder. 'All right, very strange, but I'm not quite sure why it happened. Believe it or not, I thought I was a model of sanity. Lately, though, I seem to be anything but.'

He grinned crookedly and kissed her hair. 'You are. You're also my sanity. OK, what did you want to discuss?'

Sienna took a moment to gather her thoughts, then she blushed again. Because she'd gone from having reservations about sleeping with a man because she was a virgin and not at all sure she mightn't "freeze up", to simply doing it. She had been all set to tell him that over this one thing she seemed to be a mass of contradictions, but her response to him had been anything but contradictory.

'It's really—' She stopped a little helplessly and started again, 'It's not important now, but I was going to tell you I was still a virgin, and why.'

'It doesn't make any difference to me, Sienna—well, it does,' he amended. 'It's an honour. It's—' he paused '—I feel as if you're mine alone. And that's special. Nor is it going to go away overnight. It's with us now. Isn't it?'

He looked into her eyes.

Her breathing grew ragged as she was transported back to the rapture she'd experienced in this bed and his arms only a short time ago. It was also as if a new window had been opened in her mind, one that linked her inextricably to him; a window that absorbed everything she found fascinating about him.

The way his hair grew, his lean, strong tanned hands and the thought of them on her body, the hard wall of his chest against the ripeness of her breasts.

She caught her breath because it was all so personal between them now, so intimate. She could no longer think only with her mind because, deep inside her, her body was reacting to him with a language of its own.

They "knew" each other now, she thought shakily, in the biblical sense, and nothing could ever change that.

But what about the issues that also loomed between

them? Holly Pearson and how he'd lost her, for example. Dakota and James…

'What was the nightmare about?' she asked out of the blue.

He moved away a little and rested his arm on his forehead. 'It took them a couple of hours to cut me out of the wreckage and they had to put out a fire as well, although it didn't reach me, but I was conscious all the time. It's—hard to forget.'

'Oh, Finn,' she breathed and hugged him, then stilled as she heard sounds.

'Ah, movement at the station,' he murmured, quoting Banjo Paterson, 'but—' he dropped his arm and loomed over her '—don't you dare try to escape! We've had enough interruptions and no one is going to come in here uninvited, Sienna.'

She had to smile at his look of seriousness.

'No, I won't. Finn—' She hesitated.

He walked his fingers down between her breasts and spoke rather huskily. 'I've been tormented by the perfume of your hair and skin. And just now, the way you moved in my arms—it was as if I'd trapped a free spirit. You made me think you floated on air, you were like all the elements combined, you were—' his voice deepened '—fascinating.'

She looked at him, wide-eyed. 'That's how I felt. I mean, not *fascinating*, but—'

He put a finger to her lips. 'You were.'

She sighed. 'To be honest, I'd like not to be able to award you too much credit, but I'm afraid I have to.'

He grimaced wryly, then sobered. 'Let's look at it

like this. We need each other, Sienna, that's what made it work so well, but there's more. Can you imagine being without me now? I know I can't and not only because of this but everything about you.'

Sienna closed her eyes, incredibly touched as all her objections took wings. Yes, she'd brought up his nightmare because she hadn't been able to help but think about Holly and wonder if he could ever love her as much as he'd loved Holly.

But this declaration seemed to say firmly and unequivocally that that was all in the past now.

As for her past, it occurred to her to wonder if she'd ever been madly in love with James—she'd certainly never felt like this—or if she'd subconsciously decided it was about time she fell in love otherwise she was something of a freak.

And was the sense of injury she'd suffered more because it was *Dakota* who had stolen him? Yes, she'd acknowledged it was always a thorn in her flesh, but had it been greater and deeper than she'd ever realized? A thorough, two-year fit of pique directed more towards her sister? she wondered uncomfortably.

'Penny for them?'

Her lashes fluttered up and she looked into the blue of his eyes, so intent.

The faintest smile curved her lips and she traced the blue shadows of his jaw with the tip of her finger. 'No, I can't imagine being without you now, Finn. So if you're very sure?' She paused.

'Very sure,' he said, and pulled her into his arms. 'Very, very sure.'

* * *

They got married two weeks later in a private ceremony at Waterford, although Sienna had been back to Brisbane to acquire a wedding dress.

When they'd talked about a wedding date, Finn had told her honestly that his life was due to become fairly hectic now that he was almost back to full mobility.

'I've had to put so many things off, trips I should have made and so on, so we could wait for a couple of months or we could—just do it.' He eyed her rather narrowly.

'Would I be able to come?' she queried.

'Of course, whenever you wanted to, although you might find some of it insanely boring. There's something I wanted to ask you, though. Will you want to keep on working?'

Her eyes widened. 'I hadn't thought—yes. I—I just couldn't give it all away, Finn, but naturally I'd only do it on a part-time basis and our life would always take precedence but—' She stopped and eyed him anxiously. 'I can't believe I hadn't even thought about it!'

He looked fleetingly amused. 'I can.'

'You've obviously thought about it, though,' she said slowly.

He nodded. 'In two contexts. I know how much you love it and how good you are at it. The other is—I do often get tied up with business so to know, when those inevitable times crop up that we can't be together, that you're happy and fulfilled is important.'

Her eyes softened. 'Thanks.'

'In the meantime, though, should we wait or—?' He raised his eyebrows at her.

She thought swiftly. If she'd decided to do this what

was the point of waiting? Would waiting whittle away at her and give her all sorts of agonizing second thoughts? Could she bear that?

'Let's just do it, Finn.'

He touched his fist to the point of her chin gently. 'So be it—so long as you understand there are going to be times—'

She interrupted him by repeating his gesture. She touched her fist to the point of his chin. 'Gotcha, mister!'

He grinned wickedly and captured her fist. 'Handy bunch of fives, ma'am,' he drawled.

'Happen I may never need 'em,' she responded with a cowboy twang.

'Hope not!' He looked comically apprehensive, then he disarmed her completely with a kiss that took her breath away and reassured her she was doing the right thing.

Alice overcame her aversion to cattle stations and arrived in style a week before the wedding. She immediately set the place by its ears, and if Finn and Sienna had had hopes of a small affair Alice had other ideas. She also told them Peter and Melissa Bannister were coming and Declan was coming with his latest amour; another voluptuous blonde, Alice had said with a grimace, this one named Tara.

Sienna looked a little comically perplexed at this revelation. 'That wasn't the name of the girl he was here with just—well, only a couple of weeks ago,' she ventured to Finn.

'He can change them nearly as frequently as he changes his clothes,' he replied.

* * *

They also discussed her family, now deeply immersed in Dakota's wedding—Sienna got almost daily phone calls from both her mother and sister—and she decided, much as it might break her mother's heart not to be at her own wedding, her overwhelming relief to think of her elder daughter happily married would more than compensate.

Sienna did voice one reservation to Finn, though.

'I know we decided not to wait, but if you would rather, I'd understand,' she said to him suddenly. They'd driven out to a bore and were sitting in the Land Rover watching a mob of cattle drinking as the sun set and turned the flat landscape into a rich palette of colour: gold on red, pink on deepening blue.

'Why?'

She shrugged. 'Out of respect for Holly's memory?' She was driving and she ran her hands around the steering wheel, then stopped to study her beautiful engagement ring, a circlet of tiny pearls around the most beautiful pink Argyle diamond on a gold band.

He said nothing for a time as he stared through the windscreen, then he ran his hand through his ruffled dark hair. 'No.'

'I just thought—' She stopped and concentrated on the mob as they churned the dust to mud.

Should she banish Holly from her mind now, make a vow never to raise her name again?

He turned to her. 'You just thought?'

'It was just a thought, that's all.'

'I know, and that's one of the things I like about you, Ms Torrance. You're very, very nice.'

Sienna blinked.

'Not to mention very sane.'

She looked rueful. 'Well, thanks, but—'

'Oh,' he drawled, 'there are other things I could say about you. There's the way you stretch your legs and point your toes when I touch you in certain places; there's the one certain position we adopt that really seems to please you, there is—'

'Finn,' she interrupted dangerously at the same time as she turned pink, 'don't—'

'Don't tempt you?' he countered wickedly. 'I was trying not to, as a matter of fact, out of respect for the place—we could shock those old cows silly—and the uncomfortable confines of this particular vehicle.'

She had to laugh and he put his arm over her shoulders. 'OK? You know, you've made a hit with my aunt.'

'She told me,' Sienna responded with still some surprise evident in her expression as she recalled that particular encounter, 'that I was exactly what you needed.'

'She's no fool. She's right.'

'But I thought she'd be more surprised, more…curious, or even of the opinion we should wait.'

'I think she believes I've waited long enough to have kids.'

'She did ask me if I was pregnant.'

'There you go.'

Sienna grimaced. 'Actually,' she mused, 'everyone's taken it really well. Your brother even rang me and gave me to understand that if you hadn't married me, he would have given some thought to it himself.'

'My half-brother,' Finn said after a moment on a note Sienna couldn't quite decipher.

She turned to him with a question in her eyes.

He shrugged. 'Declan is—as Declan does.'

'But you don't always approve?'

'No, I don't.' He paused. 'But it couldn't have been easy for him. I lost my father, he lost his mother as well.'

'Your aunt was pretty marvellous to him, though, by the sound of it.'

'Yes.'

Subject closed, Sienna thought, and felt a niggle of unease until he said, 'On the other hand, there's no reason I can't kiss you, is there?'

Sienna thought for a moment, then chose to answer airily, 'Only if you want to.'

He drew her towards him until their faces were inches apart. She studied the tiny white lines in the tanned skin beside his eyes, the deep blue of his irises, the way his springy dark hair grew from his forehead. She inhaled the mixture of sweat and clean cotton from his shirt. She stared at his mouth and felt her lips parting involuntarily as well as her nipples flowering…

'Say that again,' he murmured barely audibly.

She sighed. 'I have to amend it.' She raised her hand and laid her fingertips along his jaw. 'Please do.'

He smiled a lightning smile, and lowered his mouth to hers. It was almost dark before they broke apart.

That night, just before she fell asleep, Sienna remembered wondering whether now was the time to banish all thoughts of Holly Pearson, and decided that it was…

* * *

But four days before her wedding, she had a change of heart, although not about Holly.

She interrupted Finn in a conference at the rectory table about an up-coming muster; she shooed everyone away and sat down opposite him.

'I can't do it,' she said tragically.

Something like shock then a blank wall came to Finn's expression. 'Why not?'

'It's not right. I'd never forgive myself!'

'What the hell do *you* have to forgive yourself about?' he queried harshly. 'Sienna, don't be a fool.'

She blinked, then sighed. 'It may sound foolish to you, but not to me, and that's the bottom line, Finn McLeod. Incidentally,' she fired up suddenly, 'I may have agreed to marry you, but don't call me a fool. I do not, repeat not, appreciate it.'

It was Finn's turn to blink. 'But I thought you'd changed your mind about marrying me?'

She gazed at him. 'When did I say that?'

He set his teeth. 'A moment ago you said—I can't do it. Then you said, it's not right, I'd never forgive myself.'

'Yes, well, I meant it—oh!' She broke off. 'You thought—no! I meant I can't get married without my mother, my father and my sister being here—although I can do without her future husband—I just can't. So we either have to take the wedding to them or bring them here.'

Finn swore.

'I don't appreciate being sworn at either,' she said gravely, but with a sparkle of humour in her eyes. And she slid her hand across the table.

He hesitated, then put his hand on top of hers. 'You had me worried for a moment.'

'This may sound—I can't think of the right word—but I rather like the thought of that.'

'Me being worried?'

'Uh-huh.' She nodded.

'I would call that being a bit bloody-minded,' he pronounced.

Sienna picked up his hand in hers and she smiled impishly at him. 'Maybe but I'm over it now. Well—' she shrugged '—there is also this. I once reflected on the unfairness of you being able to wave a magic wand and have everyone come running.'

He raised an eyebrow. 'You did?'

'I did. It actually annoyed me very much.'

'So?' He threaded his long fingers through hers and looked at her interrogatively.

'So,' she hesitated, 'that makes it a little hard to ask this of you.'

'Why don't you let me be the judge?'

'Would you wave your magic wand and bring my parents and sister up here?' It was a serious question she posed this time.

'Fly them?'

She grimaced. 'I shudder to think of the cost involved but it's the only way I *can* think of in the short time we have left.'

'On one condition.'

She stared at him. 'What?'

'You don't let them talk you out of this, Sienna.'

'Finn, I make my own decisions now. No, I won't

let my parents do that, but I can't imagine they'd want to anyway.'

He looked sceptical. 'You don't think they might feel you've leapt into this because of Dakota and James? Or, for whatever reason, made a very hasty decision?'

'That sounds,' she said slowly and with a frown, 'as if you're playing devil's advocate, Finn.'

He clasped her hands, then released his. 'I suppose I am but from this point of view. We may know we've got all the right reasons to do it but that might not be so easy to explain to others and you may come under pressure where you're not expecting it.'

'How…' Sienna paused '…how did you explain it to Alice?'

He shrugged. 'I told her that it was what I wanted to do. Very, very much.'

'That's it?'

'Yes.'

'Finn,' Sienna said with sudden decision, 'believe me, I'm equal to the task.'

He searched her face and eyes. 'How will you explain the lateness of your invitation?'

'We didn't want to overshadow Dakota's big day, it was a late decision anyway, then we suddenly thought it would make it better for her if she didn't have to worry about me?' She raised her eyebrows. 'I don't know if we should mention we found we just couldn't wait?'

'That, actually, is all too true,' he drawled. 'I must have been mad.'

They laughed together for a moment, because it had been Finn's suggestion they not sleep together until after the wedding once everyone started arriving. She'd agreed gratefully, not that she hadn't wanted to, but she didn't want a whole houseful of people as an audience!

'It's not long now,' she offered. 'And you're not the only one suffering.'

His eyes softened on her. 'OK, let's get this show on the road.'

CHAPTER SEVEN

'HAPPY?'

Sienna looked back down her wedding day, then nodded in response to Finn's question.

It had all gone smoothly.

She'd married Finn McLeod in a long, slim white dress with single blue and white agapanthus blooms threaded through her upswept hair before a minister from Augathella who'd driven out for the ceremony.

Alice McLeod had put her heart and soul, and considerable social skills, into the buffet lunch that had followed. The event had been attended, not only by their families, but by long-time neighbours in the district and some friends Finn had flown from interstate as well as Brisbane. He'd organized that once he'd realized if he didn't do it, his aunt would.

Most importantly of all, her family—to her relief James hadn't come—had been there for her. Yes, stunned at first. Yes, just as Finn had predicted, concerned that she was marrying in haste although somewhat reassured when they discovered she'd known him for months rather than weeks.

But Dakota was the one who had gone from concern to palpable relief after she'd watched Finn and Sienna together critically.

'You really—you just seem to be a couple,' she said to Sienna in private with tears in her eyes. 'I can't tell you how much that means to me, because I didn't know if I could ever forgive myself even although—' She gestured.

'Darling, you go ahead and marry James with a clear conscience.' Sienna hugged her. 'Believe me! Just do me one favour—help Mum and Dad to see it as well.'

And perhaps the fact that they were together after two painful years had helped enormously as well, although, strangely, as her parents relaxed more and more, Dakota grew somewhat preoccupied.

Of course Finn helped with her parents. He was quiet and courteous with them. He reinforced her explanation of the dilemma they'd found themselves in and said that he hoped, they both hoped very much, that Dakota's wedding would be all the more joyous because of their own.

It must have made sense because her parents relaxed and Alice drew them into the preparations.

But her father cleared his throat, just before he led her down the gallery to give her away, and started to say, 'Sienna, sweetheart—'

'Dad,' she broke in huskily, 'it's what I really want to do.'

Ralph Torrance looked down at his elder daughter with a lot of love in his eyes. 'All the same, pet, and I'll say this to Dakota as well, if you ever need me, just give me a call.'

It had brought tears to her eyes and she'd hugged him.

* * *

The reception had been lively—Declan had seen to that aided by his current girlfriend, Tara, who, Sienna decided, she couldn't help liking. Not only was Tara very blonde and very voluptuous, she was forthright but in a rather engaging way you couldn't take offence at—she could be more outspoken than Declan himself.

'Maybe he's met his match,' she murmured to Finn as they watched Tara and Declan dance past.

Finn looked rueful. 'She's certainly quite a character.' He turned his attention back to Sienna. 'So, it's done.'

'It's done,' Sienna agreed. 'Any regrets?'

He cupped his hand around her neck and drew her forward so their foreheads were touching. 'None. How about you?'

'None,' she whispered, and he kissed her.

They'd flown away to Byron Bay where they were now installed in the honeymoon suite of a beautiful resort. And Sienna had just agreed that she was happy when, in fact, she felt exhausted, but not only physically, mentally too.

Finn brought her a glass of champagne and sat down beside her with his own glass on an emerald velvet settee. The beach and the sea—you almost felt as if you could reach out and touch them—were leached now of any sunlight; they were pale shades of grey on white as twilight fell.

'What's wrong?' he queried quietly as she stared at her glass.

She raised her eyes to his and they were bewildered and disbelieving. 'I thought I would be—I thought I would feel different. I feel—like a punching bag.'

'Have a sip,' he recommended, and when she'd done so he removed her glass and he rearranged them so she was lying in his arms. 'It's not so surprising. An awful lot of emotion has gone into the last few weeks. Relax.'

'But I should—'

'Hush,' he told her. 'There's nothing you should be doing.'

'Not even changing into something not only more comfortable but guaranteed to set you alight? Or—'

'Sienna, even you're allowed to fall apart occasionally.'

'I feel—like a wimp.'

'Actually, you feel like a tired girl and I feel like a tired guy, that's all.'

Sienna attempted to sit up. 'Your leg,' she said anxiously. 'You've had to do so much standing lately—I could give you a massage!'

He growled something indecipherable and pulled her back. 'This is all I want to be doing at the moment, Sienna Torrance, so will you just—?'

'McLeod,' she said as she subsided. 'Sienna McLeod.'

'Of course. Do you intend to follow in your parents footsteps?'

She frowned. 'How so?'

'Naming your children after their place of conception?'

A sudden gurgle of laughter shook her. 'Byron? I don't think I could do that to a boy—assuming it happened here and it was a boy. No.'

But the laughter turned inexplicably to tears and it was a while, as he held her and stroked her hair, before he felt her relax. Just before she fell asleep, he helped her up and led her to the bedroom and put her to bed. She turned away from him and fell asleep immediately.

Finn McLeod studied her thoughtfully for a long time.

To be honest, it surprised him to see the nervous tension that claimed her, that made her look pale and almost haggard. Why should it be surprising, though? he wondered. It had been a tumultuous few weeks. Had he thought she was so sane and reasonable she could handle anything?

Or did she have her own demons he knew nothing about?

He frowned suddenly and rubbed his jaw. There were some contradictions in Sienna, there had been a few surprises along the way, he recalled.

If you were an absolute cynic, he thought suddenly— and if anyone should be, he should—would you be prompted to wonder whether she'd had her own agenda right from the start? From the moment she'd thrown down the gauntlet—*Come to my sister's wedding and I'll come to Waterford?*

Had, the thought literally struck him, he been conned into this marriage? Had it all been a clever ploy, but, if so, what *was* her agenda?

He stared down at Sienna and watched her lips work in her sleep and the way her fingers clutched the pillow slip and it seemed obvious to him it was more than a taxing few weeks that was disturbing her even in her sleep.

Had she only married him to get back at her sister and James Haig? And had the enormity of what she'd done suddenly hit her?

But where did the surprising fact that she had been

a virgin fit in—unless she had another agenda entirely? Children maybe…It was plain to see she adored kids, and if you were turned off men or you'd decided you were going to carry an eternal torch for your sister's-husband-to-be…

He allowed the thought to expand in his mind. If you threw Waterford into the mix, a setting she'd taken to as if she'd been born to it, was it his seed and his cattle station she'd married him for?

It was a bizarre thought but something was obviously deeply disturbing for her…

Sienna woke the next morning and it all drifted back to her, only this time the explanation for her sudden "falling apart" was clear to her.

It had been Holly who'd trod the back roads of her subconscious from her lonely grave; Holly who'd invaded her sleep with a message along the lines of— You may have tried to put me out of your mind, but I'll always be his real love…

But why had this nemesis waited until yesterday and last night, her wedding day and night, to claim her? To cause a cold little bubble of dread to spring up so unexpectedly and even invade her sleep?

Was it that while she might have thought she'd buried all those unasked questions about Holly and the mental scars Finn must still bear, she hadn't succeeded?

And it all must have exerted more internal pressure on her than she'd realized, until finally, on top of a pressurized couple of weeks anyway, the lid had blown?

But wasn't she sane and sensible enough to realize

that Holly was gone, it was only her own, perhaps over-stretched mind playing fanciful games with her?

Or was there, behind it all, the fear that Holly might never go because she, herself, might never measure up to Holly's memory in Finn's estimation? And the fear that if she ever found that out, she'd be devastated?

She sighed and sat up. Sunlight was pouring into the room; waves were pounding on the beach.

Worse than that, it suddenly hit her that she'd not only slept right through her wedding night—she was alone.

She cast the bedclothes aside. She was wearing her underwear, that was all, so she grabbed a robe and, with it flying out behind her, hurried into the lounge.

Finn was sitting with his feet up on the coffee-table, reading the paper.

He looked over the top of it at her speedy entrance. 'Well, if it isn't Sleeping Beauty,' he drawled.

'I'm so sorry! I can't believe I did that.'

'It's certainly a good way to put a dampener on—things.'

She blushed. 'I must have been extra-tired.'

'Or bored?'

'No, of course not!' She stared at him, but he appeared to be deadly serious.

'Just wondered.' He shrugged.

'Finn—' she plaited her fingers together '—I—' she unplaited her fingers as she noticed the little glint in his eyes '—you're laughing at me!'

'Of course I'm laughing at you,' he agreed. 'Or, maybe I'm laughing at me—it's not exactly what one would like to have on one's CV. Item: sent wife to sleep on wedding night.'

'Stop it,' she begged. He was laughing openly now.

'Come here, Sienna.'

She advanced cautiously as he stood up, then walked into his arms.

'You could always make amends,' he suggested.

She rested against him, relief coursing through her. 'So you do understand?'

He looked long and deep into her eyes and she suddenly felt herself holding her breath—did he? Or—

'So long as I'm allowed to do this,' he said.

It was a deep, intoxicating kiss they shared and it led to a deeply physical encounter.

He took her back to the bedroom and he explored her body at his leisure.

'I was always a fan of your hips.' He suited actions to words as he cupped her bottom.

'What's so special about them?' she asked, with some difficulty, the result of the particular attention he'd paid to all her most erogenous spots on the way down to her hips.

'They're—jaunty.'

She had to chuckle. 'Doesn't sound very sexy!'

'Oh, they are.' He moved his hands back to her breasts.

Then he raised his head and looked at her with a faint frown. 'What?'

'I—don't know what you mean?'

'You…' he hesitated '…appeared to be struck by a sudden thought.'

She bit her lip. 'How could you tell?'

He traced the curve of her cheek. 'I just could.'

'Well, I was,' she confessed. 'I'd decided I wasn't a very sensual person.' She coloured faintly as he looked down the naked, delicately curved length of her, then back into her eyes.

He propped his head on his elbow and walked his fingers lightly down between her breasts—she loved the way he did that. 'Now you're revising that opinion?' he hazarded.

She nodded, although she looked indecisive about it. 'But it may be you.'

He laughed softly, and his hand moved lower. 'I don't subscribe to that theory.'

'How do you mean?'

'I wouldn't be here doing this unless I really wanted to, and that's got everything to do with you. So, are we of one mind in this matter?'

Sienna exhaled a shaky breath as his fingers slipped between her thighs. 'Yes…' She turned into his arms with a sigh of pleasure.

They had four wonderful days at Byron Bay.

Well, mostly wonderful, she was to think.

They drove to the lighthouse, a windy eyrie on a green-cloaked promontory, Australia's most easterly point, and witnessed a pod of humpback whales making their way south. They swam, they experienced Byron's wonderful array of eateries, art galleries and gift shops, its village atmosphere, and they sat on the beach in the moonlight.

They talked, they listened to music, they discovered some of the whimsical things that went into their personalities.

But there were times when she looked up to see him watching her with a frown in his eyes almost as if he was trying to work out some kind of puzzle. There was the odd occasion when she caught an echo in his voice she didn't understand or a *double entendre* that didn't make sense.

A couple of times she found herself wondering if the debacle of their wedding night did have more ramifications he hadn't acknowledged.

That it should come crashing down so soon after they left Byron Bay was unimaginable to Sienna, however, but that was when it did.

CHAPTER EIGHT

THEY went to Eastwood after Byron Bay because Finn had a conference to attend in Rockhampton, several hundred miles north of Brisbane in the heart of cattle country.

It was purely cattle and grazing business, he'd told her, but not something, as President of the association holding the conference, he could get out of. It would be hot in Rocky, he'd be tied up all the time, and he'd rather she didn't come.

She'd hesitated, then agreed as she'd recalled the few loose ends that still needed to be tied up from her old life. And it was only for a couple of days.

Besides which, Dakota's wedding was coming up shortly.

But he'd spent the first night with her at Eastwood and introduced her to the staff. He'd also told her, with a wry little smile, to change anything she liked or leave it all to Walt.

'Definitely my preferred option,' she murmured.

'OK.' They were saying goodbye on the veranda. 'In the meantime, don't do anything I wouldn't.' He kissed her, then paused.

'I won't.' She kissed him back and stayed in his arms for a moment longer. 'And you take care of that leg. Don't do too much in other words. I don't want you coming back as my patient. Oh, and don't forget it's Dakota's wedding on Saturday!'

'I won't—which reminds me. We've been invited to dinner the night I get home. A rather formal affair I'm afraid but it's the tenth anniversary of a joint venture I undertook with a partner that's turned out rather successfully. You'll like Marcus and his wife Liz.'

'Ah,' she said slowly. 'Formal as in black tie, long dress, et cetera?'

'Yes.' He drew his brows together. 'Is that a problem?'

She gave a sudden gurgle of laughter. 'No. I'm just thinking about my wardrobe.'

'What's wrong with it? You always look fine to me.' He smiled down at her wickedly. 'Although even better— not to put too fine a point on it—in the altogether.'

'Thanks.' She coloured deliciously and laughed a little breathlessly at the way his gaze roamed over her. 'And there's nothing wrong with it, it's just not very extensive. But that could be a pleasure to remedy,' she assured him. 'A certain amount of retail therapy always is!'

'So I've been led to believe,' he replied ruefully and he laughed down at her, his eyes very blue and very wicked, and she had to take a shaken breath because he was so—just gorgeous.

But as she watched him drive away, she experienced a niggle of unease. Was this the way her marriage was going to go? Passionate interludes in his bed and a lot of time on her own?

He had warned her about it, though, but they'd only been married for five days.

She looked back over those five days, and every unexplained little incident she'd tried to persuade herself she'd imagined rose in her mind's eye.

But once again, she made a determined effort to banish them.

She went inside and drifted through the quiet house and was tempted to pinch herself. Because six weeks ago she'd never been further than the veranda and his study and now she had the keys to it and the right to change anything she liked.

Who would want to change Eastwood, though? she wondered. She loved the blend of antiques and luxury, the high ceilings, the wide windows with their views over the gardens and down to the river.

And for more informal living, the master bedroom had a comfortable sitting room attached, a kitchenette and a secluded courtyard with outdoor furniture and an absolute riot of geraniums, impatiens, fuchsias and other pot-plants.

A clock chimed softly somewhere and she glanced at her watch. Time to get doing things, she decided, but first she would unpack properly, something she hadn't had time to do the day before.

She smiled as she made herself a cup of coffee in the kitchenette and took it into the bedroom. The housekeeper had actually offered to unpack for her but she'd declined—perhaps that was something she would need to get used to? Someone on hand to do just about everything for her?

She'd met the housekeeper who was also the cook,

the two cleaners who came in daily, the gardener who cared for the pool as well and the laundress who came twice a week.

A high number of staff for one man, she reflected—there was also Walt to oversee it all, but it was during Walt's tour of the house with her that she came to understand why.

It was a large old house that took a lot of caring for, for it to sparkle the way it did.

'We wash all the crystal and china once a month,' Walt said, 'whether it's been used or not. Dust can play havoc with it and a lot of it is old and valuable so it has to be done by hand. But we do use it a lot. We entertain frequently and it's always of the highest standard.' She was to get used to Walt's royal "we". 'There's also a lot to polish, furniture, silver and so on. And we frequently have guests staying overnight—that creates a lot of laundry.'

He hesitated then before going on. 'Mrs Lawson—' Mrs Lawson was the housekeeper '—would be more than happy to assist you with the maintenance of your wardrobe, but if you'd prefer someone else I could look out for someone suitable.'

If she hadn't been afraid of shocking Walt, she would have replied immediately that her wardrobe, as it stood, was perfectly easy to maintain single-handedly, but perhaps that needed to change? she wondered.

In the end she told him that she'd consult Mrs Lawson herself in the next few days.

The master bedroom was pure indulgence. A cool wooden floor, hand-woven rugs, dusky blue walls and the lovely subtle use of blues and greys with the odd flash of magenta. The bed was not only king-sized, but a four-poster with a cloud-like grey chiffon canopy and a striking silver wall hanging behind it studded with semi-precious stones. An exquisite cream bow-fronted French colonial chest of drawers stood along one wall with two Georgian silver candlesticks on it and a bowl of pink and blue hydrangeas.

And there were not one but two *en suite* bathrooms, his and hers.

The dressing room was a marvel of organization, drawers that worked perfectly, she discovered as she unpacked, shelves, cupboards, storage for suitcases, shoe racks and the woodwork was curiously fragrant—camphor wood, she decided. Of course she had a lot more of her clothes to bring from her apartment, plus her special things, and a decision to be made about her furniture.

Those were some of the things she intended to address today and tomorrow.

She was hanging up the last item from her luggage, a dress with a belt, when the slim belt, not properly looped into its carriers, parted company with the dress and slithered down behind a shoe rack.

She had to get down on her hands and knees, but she couldn't even see it until she realized the rack came out in a separate piece rather like an open-fronted bookshelf with a back and a rod across it.

She slid it out and fished out her belt from behind it, as well as a slip of paper.

She smoothed it open, could see immediately it

wasn't Finn's writing, then her jaw dropped as she read the round, flamboyant hand. It said:

> *Don't think you can do this to me, Finn, I will not be brushed aside. Laura made a fool of your father. Do you want that spread all over the papers? Oh, and there's more.*

It was signed; *'Holly'*.

She got to her feet after a stunned few moments and carried the note to the bedroom where she sank down on the bed and reread it, but it made no more sense than the first time she'd read it.

Unless, she thought incredulously, Finn and Holly Pearson *hadn't* been the perfect couple, and how could they have been if Holly was blackmailing him over— what?

Laura was Declan's mother—did this have something to do with Declan? Did it explain the *unexplained* rift between Finn and Declan? But how?

Her eyes dilated as she stared out towards the sun-splashed courtyard, only it seemed to have lost its brightness.

She put her hand to her chest and left it there for a moment. Then she swallowed and commanded herself to think straight and concentrate on what it meant to *her*.

And what immediately occurred to her was that, at times, she'd wondered about Finn and Holly herself. She could even recall the very first time she'd been moved to wonder; the first time they'd discussed her going to Waterford. She had thought about patient attachment, he'd asked her if she was afraid he was falling in love with her, then gone on to say something about when you've had the best, it wasn't going to happen again.

But it was the way he'd said it that had drawn a puzzled internal response from her—she remembered it so well—as if she'd felt the prick of a pin she hadn't known was there. Of course she'd immediately rationalized it, put it down to his still being bereft, but could it have been something else? Could he and Holly have *not* been the perfect couple for some reason?

Two other things flooded her mind as she thought along these lines. The fact that a wedding would be the last thing she'd expect him to want to go to—when she'd stopped to think!—when his own wedding had been in the planning stage before those tragic events.

The fact that he didn't seem to care if his name was linked to another woman so relatively soon after Holly's death, or, come to that, that he would want to marry another woman so soon...

She put her hands to her head—talk about a Pandora's box! What were the implications of it? Why hadn't Finn told her the truth?

But what was worse—to discover that Holly Pearson had not been the love of his life or the fact that he hadn't confided in her?

The phone beside the bed buzzed discreetly.

She picked it up. 'Hello?'

'Miss McLeod is here to see you, Miss—Mrs McLeod,' Walt said down the line.

'Oh, thank you. I'll—I'll come.' Sienna stood up and

pushed the note into her pocket, and she hurried into the bathroom to tidy her hair and wash her hands.

Alice was ensconced in the lounge but she got up to greet Sienna with a hug. Then she frowned. 'How are you? You look a bit pale.'

'I'm fine. And you look wonderful!'

Alice did in a powder blue suit with her cap of white hair shining and ordered. 'I'm off to a charity luncheon,' she said with a grimace, however, 'but I heard you were alone so I came over for a chat. I've also got some wedding photos.'

So they went through the photos, reminiscing pleasantly about the wedding until they came to one of Declan and Tara, and Alice paused to sigh in a rather heartfelt way. 'I just wish Declan would find someone as nice as you, Sienna.'

'Thank you.' Sienna smiled at her, then she said carefully, 'I rather liked Tara. I even thought they made a good pair.'

Alice looked pained. 'Somewhat lacking in class, wouldn't you say? Perfectly suited to be in a B grade movie, perhaps, but otherwise?'

'Oh—'

But Alice steamed on, 'The problem is, Declan has an inferiority complex. Living up to Finn hasn't been easy. Of course he never had the responsibilities Finn has had from a relatively early age, but even when we did delegate some of it to Declan, well, probably the least said there, the better.'

Sienna stared at her.

'Then there's the fact that his mother was—I have to concede—gorgeous in a rather flashy kind of way, but there was very little substance to her. That aside, though—I do not believe in visiting the sins of parents upon their children otherwise I would never have taken Declan on—despite my best efforts, there are times—' she shook her head '—when I can't help wondering if Declan goes out of his way to be outrageous just to annoy Finn.'

'But they're—I mean, sibling rivalry aside, they have to be close in a way, don't they?' Sienna asked disjointedly as the circles of her mind tumbled like a fruit machine.

Alice ran her beautifully manicured fingernails on the arm of her chair. 'There may always be a deep rift between those two, my dear. Yes, they gloss over it, but it's there.' She gestured suddenly. 'Naturally, I would never discuss this outside the family, but you are family now and to be honest this—this woman—'

'Tara.'

'Whatever her name is and the way Declan is *flaunting* her at me is—very annoying.'

Sienna drew a breath. 'Alice—' she'd been invited to call her aunt-in-law by her first name '—I think you should just go with the flow. If Declan is deliberately trying to annoy you or Finn—as a matter of fact I don't think Finn has thought much about it at all, but if Declan is, when he gets no response, he'll desist.'

Alice grimaced. 'Of course you're right!' She gathered up the photos, then looked around. 'Have you decided to make any changes? I grew up here, you know, in between stints on cattle stations.' She looked heavenwards.

Sienna smiled. 'No, no changes in mind. I think it's lovely as it is.'

'Holly would have—' Alice stopped abruptly.

'Would she?' Sienna simply couldn't help herself, but she added, 'Of course, I didn't know her.' She shrugged.

'Holly had a habit of imprinting herself on everything. Other people's ideas didn't suit her at all. I was always rather amazed she set her cap at Finn. He is definitely not the kind of man you can dominate, but of course his fortune was another matter. Is he OK?' Alice asked suddenly.

'Fine,' Sienna said steadily.

'Don't mind me.' Alice stood up. 'I'm probably an interfering old spinster, but I'm not inexperienced,' she said, 'and I'm not blind. So I do know that some things can't be easy for you. But don't for one minute imagine you're living in Holly's shadow because I'm of the opinion you're much better for Finn than she ever was. Now give me a kiss and I'll take myself off!'

Sienna retreated to the informal sitting room after Alice's departure with her mind still going round in circles.

It was not hard to read between the lines—Alice hadn't liked Holly, hadn't thought she was right for Finn, had even suggested Holly was manipulative.

But did Alice, at the same time, believe Finn would never get over Holly? Why else would she have asked how he was? Why else had she issued an oblique but nonetheless little statement that could have been understood to read—Hang in there, Sienna?

Then there was Declan. How difficult must it have been

for Declan McLeod to be brought up by his father's sister? Wasn't it inevitable that *some* of Alice's disapproval of his mother would leach through despite her denials?

On top of that, to have an older half-brother who was a model of everything he, Declan, wasn't—would that be enough to turn Declan against Finn? All the same, what part *had* Declan played that had brought about Holly's note and did it have something to do with the rift between him and Finn?

Then a thought struck her. Instead of worrying about all the things she didn't understand, shouldn't she be jumping for joy because, although Alice might not have known it, Finn had, at the least, fallen out of love with Holly Pearson? Surely if Holly had been blackmailing him he must have?

She stared down at her hands and saw that they were shaking, and she couldn't doubt it was the power of her emotions for Finn and the relief of this revelation.

She only had to think of him now to know that he was part of her heart and soul. To know that to lose him would be a blow she didn't think she could bear.

But why hadn't he told her? Because he truly believed the past was better left unsaid?

They talked on the phone that night and when they ended the call she felt reassured that everything was the same between them, at least as it had been when he'd left.

And she went to sleep with the thought on her mind that she really should put it all away from her because one day, when he was ready, Finn would tell her the truth about Holly…

CHAPTER NINE

'THERE'S someone to see you, Mrs McLeod.'

Sienna jumped.

She was sitting on the master suite's private patio enjoying the early sunshine before it got too hot. Finn was due home that afternoon. She'd spoken to him again this morning, a conversation mostly to do with how she'd packed up her old life.

She turned to see Mrs Lawson standing behind her.

'Oh, thank you. Who is it?'

'A Mr Haig.'

'Haig?' Sienna repeated incredulously.

Mrs Lawson nodded. 'He's waiting in the lounge. He said it was rather urgent.'

Sienna got up hurriedly, her mind running along the lines of—had something happened to her parents or Dakota? Or was the name a sheer coincidence?

It wasn't. It was the instantly recognizable tall back of James Haig in the lounge as he stared out over the river.

'James?' Fear and uncertainty made her voice extra husky. 'What's happened? Why are you here?'

He turned convulsively. He had curly brown hair and

hazel eyes, he was undeniably good-looking and he wore a charcoal business suit with a blue shirt and a navy tie. He looked every inch the successful stockbroker he was except for his expression, which was distraught.

'Sienna, she wants to cancel the wedding!'

Sienna gasped. 'Dakota? But why?'

'She says you made her understand we just didn't have what it takes. What did you tell her?' he demanded.

'N-nothing,' Sienna stammered. 'All I told her was to go ahead and marry you with a clear conscience.'

'I can't believe that. There must be something else but whatever, you've got to talk to her, Sienna. It's only a few days away. What on earth are people going to think? How could she do this to me?'

'Is that all you're worried about?'

'All!' he said. 'Isn't it enough? But, Sienna—' he strode over to her and took her shoulders in his hands '—you've got to talk to her. *Please.*'

'I—'

'If you still feel anything for me, and I think you must otherwise you wouldn't have rushed into marrying Finn McLeod, please,' he insisted.

The last scales fell from Sienna's eyes in relation to James Haig. Why had she not seen the shallowness of this man right from the start? Why had she tormented herself over him for so long?

But to her horror he then took her in his arms and said again, 'Please, Sienna!'

'Please what?' someone queried dryly from the doorway. Finn.

James released her and they both spun round.

Finn wore a khaki bush shirt, jeans and short boots and he dropped his bag and his cattleman's hat to the floor.

'Finn, I wasn't expecting you until this afternoon!' Sienna rushed into speech. 'But Dakota wants to call off the wedding and James wants me to speak to her—uh—this is James Haig. James, Finn McLeod.'

The two men eyed each other.

'Well, well,' Finn drawled, and strolled up to Sienna's side. 'The worm has turned, by the look of it.'

James thrust his jaw out. 'What's that supposed to mean?'

'I should have thought it was obvious. You dumped Sienna for Dakota, now Dakota has dumped you. Incidentally, I don't appreciate you importuning my wife in this manner, so please let Dakota speak for herself. In the meantime, I'll see you out.'

Sienna stood transfixed as she saw James about to launch himself at Finn, but he was stared down in such a formidable manner he thought better of it, and, with only a savage broadside to the effect that he'd see himself out, he left.

'You didn't want him to stay, by any chance?' Finn queried, his blue eyes still hard and hostile as he turned back to her.

'No. I mean, no, but—' She stopped helplessly.

'What I can't understand is why he would come to you in the first place?'

For some reason Sienna's tongue tripped her up.

'She is—she is my sister. She—' She stopped and started again. 'She told him, apparently, that I'd made her see it wouldn't work between them.'

'Did you?'

'No! Of course not. Finn—' she frowned '—what is this?'

'Rough justice?' he reflected. 'Perhaps you bore more of a grudge against James Haig than you let on? I don't know, but getting her to call it off four days before the wedding is inspired revenge.'

Sienna took a mighty lungful of air and slapped his face.

He grabbed her wrist and for a terrified moment she thought he was going to retaliate. But the glare in his eyes was suddenly replaced by biting irony. 'A handy bunch of fives, after all, but perhaps I should warn you to keep them to yourself in future. So—' his eyes narrowed '—I seem to have hit a nerve. You're the last person I would have suspected of being a face-slapper.'

Sienna grappled with a sense of shame—she'd never slapped anyone in her life—but her anger was still there.

'How could you say that? How could you *believe* that of me?' Sudden tears stood in her eyes.

He shrugged and dropped her wrist. 'It just made me wonder how absolutely open and up front you are, Sienna.'

She opened and closed her mouth but was essentially speechless.

'But, anyway, is this damn wedding on or off?' he grated.

'We shall see,' she said precisely. 'Would there be a remote phone in this house?'

'Of course,' he replied impatiently.

'Then you listen in on it while I make a call.'

* * *

Some minutes later, Sienna ended her call, not to her sister, but her mother.

The gist of it was that Dakota had called the wedding off but not only that, she'd flown the coop.

'But why? Mum, please stop crying, this is important!'

'I don't know,' her mother wept. 'All she would say was that it was *you* who made her see things straight!'

'But I didn't. It was the opposite, if anything! Where's she gone?'

But her mother didn't know, amongst a great many other things she didn't know, such as how you could get so close to marrying a man then call it off; such as what to do with the guests who were away or incommunicado for whatever reason—and on and on, until Sienna said she would have to ring her back.

Sienna put the phone down and looked frustratedly across at Finn.

They were in his study, sitting on opposite sides of his desk.

'What did you say to her, Sienna?' he queried.

'I told her to go ahead and marry him with a clear conscience, that's all. So you have a choice, Finn. You can believe me—or not.' Her throat worked as she grappled with this nightmare—how *could* things have changed between them like this?

'If you'd come home and discovered me in the arms of another woman, what would you believe?' he countered, and smiled dryly. 'That something rather peculiar was going on?'

'No…' Sienna had to clear her throat. 'No, things can't turn on the head of a pin like that, Finn!'

'I heard him say you must still feel something for him. Why would he say that, Sienna?' His eyes were hostile again and challenging, and he didn't wait for a reply. 'Incidentally, things *can* turn on the head of a pin. It's happened to me before.' He stood up abruptly.

'Finn, I can't believe this is happening to us! Please don't—'

But he interrupted her again. 'You know, I wondered if you had your own demons, Sienna, or your own skeletons in the cupboard. It was always rather a—weird gauntlet to toss down at me: *Come to the wedding and I'll come to Waterford.* Then there was the state you were in on your wedding night.'

She gasped. 'That had nothing to do with James or Dakota!'

'No?' He leant his fists on the desk and his voice was sardonic as he continued. 'No regrets because whatever you do you can't forget James Haig? What was it, then?'

Her lips parted on the truth, but she hesitated. Hadn't she had enough flung back in her face? Hadn't she in essence been called a liar? What would he do with her admission that she hadn't known how she would cope if she failed to measure up to Holly—throw that back at her too?

'I was over-tired.'

'You? Over-tired?' he mocked her. 'You have more energy than just about anyone I know, Sienna.'

'You seemed to accept it at the time!' She broke off and bit her lip.

'Which just about says it all,' he murmured as he scanned her disturbed expression.

She snapped suddenly. She thrust back her chair and

stood up. 'That's enough, Finn! Think what you like but don't come near me in this mood.'

'I wasn't proposing to,' he drawled. 'However, we are married and that's the way we'll stay until I say otherwise.' He turned away and turned back. 'So don't plan on going anywhere, Sienna, until we sort this all out. And don't forget we have a dinner to go to tonight.' He walked out.

Her mouth fell open in disbelief and an uprush of anger consumed her. That was exactly what she would do, she decided, go away, because she refused to be treated like this.

But moments later a mental vision came to her. All her possessions that she'd decided to keep, she'd boxed and had sent to Eastwood, where they now stood in a storeroom.

The rest of it, her furniture, she'd sold *en masse* to a second-hand furniture dealer and would, probably by now, have been collected leaving her apartment empty—she could see it in her mind's eye, empty and forlorn. Not only that, she'd sublet the lease on the apartment so it was no longer hers, she'd signed the papers yesterday.

But why should she go anywhere? she suddenly wondered.

Wasn't that like admitting defeat or looking guilty when she'd done nothing, absolutely nothing?

At that point, she heard Finn drive off and she sat down again, claimed by sheer disbelief and shaken to the core so that her legs felt quite wobbly.

Then she decided to ring her mother back as she'd

promised, but she got her father; he'd made her mother lie down. But he didn't know any more and even her sane, rational father was bemused.

Sienna recounted her conversation with Dakota before her wedding, finishing, 'That's all, Dad, I swear, although…' she paused and thought back '…she was a bit emotional but I thought it was happiness. For me, for her and James. But then—and then she did seem a bit withdrawn.'

Her father sighed down the line. 'I guess Dakota has always been a law unto herself, Sienna, and better for it to have happened now rather than later. Don't worry, I'll pick up the pieces. How are you, pet?'

'Fine,' Sienna lied. 'Just fine, Dad!'

But she was anything but fine when she put the phone down, and on an impulse she grabbed her purse and her car keys, and she drove away from Eastwood with no clear intention other than to get away for a while.

It wasn't far down Hamilton Hill to Kingsford-Smith Drive, that ran along the river, and the new Brisbane Cruise Terminal at Portside Wharf. She turned into the wharf, again on an impulse, having never seen it, and not much later she was having a cup of coffee in the very up-market precinct.

There were no cruise ships in port but plenty of visitors enjoying the shopping, the eating, the Port of Brisbane Visitors' Centre, and the river.

But her mind didn't stray far from everything that had happened to her for long, and it struck her that she not only felt desperately hurt, she felt powerless and as if she was surrounded by the unknown. Nothing made sense, in other words, least of all why the man she loved should turn into a hostile stranger.

I've got to find the truth behind all this, she thought, but where to start? Could—she went still—could it all lead back to the note from Holly she'd found, somehow?

She sat for over an hour in a brown study unable to find any answers other than that strange feeling Holly's letter played a significant part, then she got up to wander through the shops listlessly.

It was, of all things, a turquoise dress that brought her out of her reverie. She stared at it and, on an indrawn breath, decided she had to have it for tonight despite the fact that she'd decided not to indulge in any retail therapy for this dinner. And almost immediately she reminded herself she wasn't sure she would be going anywhere with Finn tonight and how could she be thinking of clothes at a time like this anyway?

Because some women turned to chocolates in crisis times, some turned to shopping?

No, she decided. It was because she needed a presence if she was going out with Finn tonight, a sophisticated, dressed-just-right presence because—she squared her shoulders resolutely—if she found out nothing else tonight, she intended to find out why Holly Pearson should have been blackmailing Finn.

For which she would require all her poise and composure.

Finn came home half an hour before they were due to leave.

Sienna was still in her bathroom putting the finishing touches to herself when she heard him come in and heard his bathroom door close.

She blotted her lips carefully, applied another layer of lipstick then some lip-gloss and took one last look at herself.

She would do, she decided, and also decided to wait for Finn in the lounge. She picked up her silver beaded evening purse on the way through the bedroom.

She was standing at the lounge windows looking down at the river when she heard him come in behind her.

She drew a careful breath and turned slowly, but the sight of him all but took that breath away because Finn McLeod in a dinner suit, black bow tie and pleated white shirt was magnificent.

The black and white austerity plus the beautiful tailoring of the suit made him look even taller and added a note of another-age mystery to him, so that she thought with a pang that he would have made a perfect rake...

Then he raised an eyebrow at her and took her in, in every detail.

The dress was exquisite, she knew. Timelessly elegant and off-the-shoulder, it sculpted her figure in beautiful turquoise lace over a taffeta lining. Silver sandals peeped out from below it. She wore her hair swept back on one side and secured with a diamante-encrusted comb. The strategic use of a turquoise eyeliner and soft silver eye-shadow accentuated her grey eyes and she'd used a hint of blusher on her smooth skin to counteract the fact that she was paler than normal.

In any other circumstances she would have felt good, not the bundle of nerves she was.

'Well,' he drawled, 'considering I wasn't altogether expecting you to make this appearance, it would seem you've gone the other way. You look stunning, Sienna.'

'Thank you.' She looked away, but proudly.

'That's all?'

'For the moment, yes,' she replied evenly.

'That sounds ominous,' he commented after a moment. 'You may as well tell me now.' He shot back his cuff and glanced at his watch. 'We have five minutes.'

Sienna gritted her teeth, then forced herself to count all the way to ten. 'No, Finn. This is going to be hard enough as it is. Let's just get it over and done with.'

'I am surprised you didn't do a bunk,' he said. 'If you feel so strongly about things.'

'Oh, I do,' she assured him. 'But I'm not the bunking type.' Sheer anger glinted in her eyes as she gazed at him.

He appeared to debate for a moment, then he shrugged and gestured. 'After you, Mrs McLeod.'

There were nightmares and nightmares, Sienna decided, halfway through the evening.

And, unlike most, this one could hardly have taken place in lovelier circumstances.

Marcus and Liz Hawthorn lived at Cleveland right on the shores of Moreton Bay in a huge house that was lit up like a birthday cake. Not only that, there were fairy lights and flaming braziers in the garden and, almost as if it had been ordered, a full moon was hanging in the sky over the bay, turning the waters platinum along its path.

There were at least fifty guests and the women could have made up a bouquet of flowers in their gorgeous gowns. There was a sit-down dinner by candlelight on the broad veranda. When that was cleared away and some speeches made, a cake in the shape of the number ten and decorated with sparklers was wheeled out and cut ceremonially as champagne corks popped.

Not exactly the stuff nightmares were made of and, indeed, Sienna had been welcomed enthusiastically especially by her hosts, who'd gone out of their way to make her comfortable.

It should have been an enjoyable evening, but the task of playing a happy new bride was the most taxing she'd ever undertaken, although, to give him his due, Finn played his part. He didn't leave her side. But that was a far cry from their "togetherness" at their wedding, for example, for anyone who knew what to look for.

Alice was there as well as Declan and Tara, although Alice didn't look especially thrilled about that. For some reason Declan didn't look particularly pleased about anything, causing Sienna to wonder, with a sense of irony, if both the McLeod half-brothers were having difficulties with their love lives.

But things got really difficult when the two-piece band struck up.

'Shall we dance, Sienna?' Finn held out his hand to her.

'I didn't know you were dancing!' She bit her lip immediately.

'I'm not, but would you call this kind of sedate shuffle dancing?'

'Well, not exactly.'

'And if we're to continue this charade why not get it out of the way, then I can claim that's all my leg is up to?'

She looked into his eyes and they were so scathing she flinched as if she'd been branded. But what to do? And why—oh, why!—had she come tonight?

'All right,' she said stiffly, and moved into his arms.

They moved in silence to the slow, dreamy beat for a few minutes as the dance floor laid on the grass under the stars and moon filled up.

Then Finn said barely audibly, 'You may not want to be dancing with me, but there's no need to feel quite so wooden in my arms.'

She stumbled but he steadied her and pulled her closer. 'Considering how much more intimate we've been,' he added. 'Only days ago when I touched you in a certain spot—' he sent a lightning glance down her body '—the way you reacted was rather cataclysmic. Or—' he raised an eyebrow at her '—is all the brilliant acting you've been doing getting a bit much?' He let his fingers wander over her bare shoulder.

'On the other hand,' he continued, 'at least I succeeded where James Haig failed, unless you'd decided to keep yourself for him until there didn't seem to be any point?'

'W-what are you saying?' she breathed, her eyes anguished.

'I'm just exploring all the angles.' He swung her

around gently to the music and his lips twisted into a mocking little smile.

'No,' she whispered, 'you're being diabolical doing this to me on a dance floor amongst a whole lot of people!'

'A thorough bastard?' he suggested and shrugged. 'Maybe, and maybe it was seeing my wife in another man's arms, who knows? Perhaps I should have told you, Sienna, that I required absolute faithfulness from you. No,' he said as she tried to free herself, 'we will leave this party shortly but together and in a dignified manner. There,' he said as the tune ended and they came to a standstill. 'Why don't you get your purse and I'll set the farewells up?'

'I—I—'

'Off you go,' he said with a kind of lethal gentleness that was terrifying.

They said not a word to each other on the drive home and if she was still pale and shaken, he was pale and grim.

And after they'd garaged the car, he followed her into the house a bit like a prison warder; he even directed her into the lounge when she would have gone towards their informal sitting room.

'Sit down,' he said, but before he sat himself he poured two brandies into balloon glasses and handed her one.

She watched his wrists and hands, of all things, as she accepted her glass. She'd always found them especially appealing to her and it amazed her that they could still send a little shiver through her.

Then she took a sip of brandy—she badly needed

it—but she immediately put the glass down and gathered all the composure she could.

'Finn,' she said quietly, 'was Holly the love of your life?'

He hadn't sat down, he'd walked over to the windows to stare down towards the river, that riveting view it was almost impossible to resist.

But Sienna found herself thinking suddenly—I hate those windows, I hate that view of the river, I'll always associate it with trauma! as he turned to her with a frown.

'What the hell has that got to do with anything?' He walked back to stand in front of her.

'I don't know,' she conceded. 'But it struck me there has to be something going on I don't understand—and maybe it goes back to this.' She opened her purse and pulled out the note.

'You see,' she went on, 'it just doesn't make sense for you to mistrust me so badly over a set of circumstances I had no control over.'

'Sienna,' he said grimly, 'you *were* the one who was a bundle of nerves on your wedding night as if you had a whole cupboard full of demons to deal with. You were instrumental, according to James Haig, and your *mother*, in getting Dakota to call her wedding off.'

'And you're the one who is choosing to take their word over mine,' she said through a clogged throat. 'Which, particularly in light of this—' she smoothed the note open '—made me wonder if something like this had happened to you before. Please read this.' She handed him the note and explained where she'd found it.

He went perfectly still as he scanned the piece of

paper, then he shut his teeth hard and crumpled it into a ball and pushed it into his pocket. When he looked at her, his eyes were as bleak as shadowed blue ice.

'Oh, yes, Sienna, you've got it in a nutshell,' he said sardonically. 'I have been through this before, that's probably why I'm a bit sensitive about manipulative women. She was good at that.'

'Tell me,' Sienna pleaded.

He hesitated, then sat down opposite her. 'She got just about everyone who knew her in, me included, but it so happens she got Declan in first.' He sat forward with his balloon glass cradled in his hands. 'She somehow managed to disguise the fact that she had the morals of an alley cat and she wasn't above stooping to blackmail to cover her tracks. She had an affair with Declan, something I didn't know anything about, before I met her.'

He paused.

'Then Declan was relatively small fish compared to you?' Sienna suggested.

He nodded. 'But Declan was bitter about being dumped for me. He threatened to tell me and he told her that once I knew, I wouldn't touch her with a bargepole. That's when she started to blackmail him.'

'How?'

He rolled the glass in his hands, then took a sip of brandy. 'Declan's mother didn't have a good reputation, unbeknownst of course to my father. Holly's mother had been a friend of hers and apparently it had always been the subject of gossip—was Declan my father's son? Holly went a step further, she told Declan he wasn't but if he'd keep quiet about their affair, she would return the favour.'

'And he believed her?' Sienna asked, wide-eyed.

'At first he did.' Finn paused again and sighed. 'Look, you've got to understand there's always been a sort of rivalry between us. I couldn't help resenting Laura, I didn't want a stepmother or a half-brother, I couldn't help feeling my mother's devastation. I still can't relate to Declan's playboy ways or his complete lack of business acumen. But I have to acknowledge that growing up in my shadow wouldn't have been easy for him.'

'I did wonder about that,' Sienna murmured.

'Yes, well, that and the fact that we're so different probably all contributed to Declan seeing it as a possibility. On top of that, naturally, the thought of being dispossessed as a McLeod was not a pleasant one. It was probably terrifying. And he did keep quiet for a time. Anyway, Holly tossed him the odd favour behind my back.' He broke off and stared broodingly down at his glass.

'But when we got engaged,' he went on, 'he got mad and one day he got drunk. He said something about Holly that could only have come from a man who'd slept with her. We—' he looked away '—had strong words—and all the rest of it came out.'

'Did—did it make sense to you immediately?' Sienna queried.

'I could not imagine Declan offering the information to me that we weren't related under any circumstances other than the truth,' Finn said precisely. 'Of course Holly denied it. She said Declan had tried to move in on her *after* she and I had met but she'd vigorously repulsed him.

'But you know—' he stopped and stared into the distance '—that's when I saw something in her I didn't like. She was too quick on the draw, too…practised about it.' He looked away with a grimace. 'I also got some tests rushed through, Declan is my legitimate heir. So I called it off. That's when she fell into her own trap. That's when she tried to blackmail me.' He patted his pocket. 'That's when she sent me the note. I decided to meet her for one last time to tell her she was wasting her time. That's when—the accident happened.'

'She sounds like—pure poison,' Sienna said unsteadily, then her eyes dilated. 'How could you compare me to her?'

Finn looked away. 'Do you think I haven't asked myself a million times how I could have been so taken in by Holly?' he said harshly. 'I ignored Alice on the subject— I put her aversion down to the fact that Holly wasn't good with other women, but the truth was I got taken in by an extremely manipulative—' He shook his head.

'But that means,' Sienna reasoned, 'that means you're never going to trust me because of *her*. That's insane.' She sprang up.

'Is it?' he queried. 'Clichés tend to be frowned upon—maybe because they hit a nerve?' He shrugged. 'The fact remains, once bitten twice shy.'

She was pale to her lips now. 'So, for the rest of our lives, on the flimsiest of pretexts, you're going to suspect me of heaven knows what? Oh, no, Finn!'

'Flimsy?' he drawled. 'Why *did* you marry me, Sienna?'

Her lips worked but nothing came out.

'Are we two of a kind?' he said then. 'Both living a lie? You can't forgive him but you can't forget him; I could never forgive her but I certainly, by omission but all the same, have lied about that.'

Sienna tried to sort through it all but she was too dazed to be able to think coherently—apart from one question that seemed to be hammering at her.

'Why did *you* marry me, Finn?'

The question stood stark in the quiet night air, then he said slowly, 'You seemed to be the antithesis of Holly, Sienna, and it seemed to be very important to find someone who would never remind me of her.'

'But now—' silent tears poured down her cheeks '—you think I also have feet of clay?'

He drained the last of his brandy and put his glass down and said with his head bent, 'What did you say to Dakota? Why did you change your mind at the last minute about getting her to *our* wedding?' He looked up at last. 'You seemed to be quite sure the best way to do it was to do it secretly, then…' He gestured. 'What happened to make you change your mind?'

Her shoulders slumped. 'Nothing,' she wept, and brushed her tears away with her fingers. Then she took hold. 'But since you won't believe me, here's what I suggest. That I pack up and leave tomorrow—actually, it's not a suggestion, it's what I'll be doing and nothing will make me change my mind,' she warned.

He looked her up and down. 'Why don't you stay and fight? Why don't you track Dakota down—?'

'Why don't you, Finn?' she broke in, 'Since you don't believe a word I say?'

'OK.' He stood up and shoved his hands into his pockets. 'I will. On one condition. You stay put while I do.'

'Finn, how can we live in the same space when we're like sworn enemies?' she cried.

'Or are you afraid of what Dakota might tell me?' he challenged.

'No! I—'

'Then stay, Sienna,' he ground out. 'It's my only offer—and I won't be here anyway.'

Her eyes widened. 'Where? I mean…' She trailed off awkwardly.

'There's a business trip to Perth I can bring forward now the wedding is off. I'll go tomorrow. Far enough away?' he queried with a dry little smile.

She couldn't say anything.

He shrugged. 'Beside which you told me your apartment had gone.'

'Yes…But how will you track Dakota down from Perth?'

He grimaced. 'I don't propose to hotfoot it around after her personally.'

'No!' Sienna said with sudden decision. 'She's got to be upset enough as it is without a posse of private detectives trying to trace her!'

'No?' he repeated. 'You really don't want me to get to Dakota, do you?'

Sienna nearly screamed in frustration. 'I just don't want her harassed,' she said through her teeth.

He frowned. 'You show an awful lot of concern for a sister who seems to have done nothing but bring you a lot of heartache but—she won't be, I promise. You should go to bed,' he added.

'A—' Her voice cracked. 'Alone?'

A ghost of humour lit his eyes. 'Probably a good idea in the circumstances. I'll do the decent thing, use a spare bed.'

Sienna closed her eyes briefly because it was like confronting a battering ram; no, she thought, a man walled into his memories, and it was a wall she simply couldn't break through but—did she even want to?

'Thanks,' she said and turned away. She managed to walk out surprisingly steadily.

CHAPTER TEN

FINN left after breakfast the next morning, but it was tense and uncomfortable for Sienna as their paths crossed inevitably before he did so.

He was cool but polite, she was only able to answer in monosyllables and she knew she looked pale and ill—she felt ill.

But when he stopped once and studied her narrowly, then asked her if she was going to be OK, she merely looked at him with disbelief tinged with scorn and turned away.

And after he'd gone, because she knew she'd go crazy sitting alone and reliving it all, she almost rang Peter Bannister to explain that she'd like to come back to work part-time since Finn had an awful lot on his plate at the moment, but something held her back.

Because it was going to sound strange when they'd been married for little over a week? Probably, she decided.

But when, a little later, her queasy feeling translated itself into reality—she lost what little breakfast she'd been able to eat in a painful interlude—another possibility struck her and nearly caused her to faint.

She was—she couldn't be!—but of course she could be pregnant because after their first unprotected act of love-making they'd decided not to wait to start a family...

Finn was drinking coffee and studying some documents.

They'd taken off half an hour ago and the plane had now levelled out. He glanced out of the window but there was a layer of cloud below them so nothing to see but clear sunlit air.

Was it raining at Waterford? he wondered, and thought back to the last time it had rained there, and Sienna, covered in mud, and stamping her foot at him...

It was no great leap to picture her pale shuttered face as he'd last seen it.

He gritted his teeth. Would he ever lose the feeling generated on their wedding night that she was not the open, honest girl he'd taken her for? Then have that disquiet fed—ballooned would be more accurate, he thought grimly—by discovering her in James Haig's arms and learning she'd caused Dakota to call off the wedding?

But where was their marriage going to go from this impasse?

And why did he suddenly have a gut feeling something was wrong?

He examined it from all angles but he couldn't identify it other than it was something to do with Sienna, and it wouldn't go away.

He swung his tray table aside, pushed himself out of his seat and strode up to the cockpit. 'Turn back, mate,' he said to the pilot. 'I've had a change of plan.'

'But—but—'

'Just do it,' Finn ordered. 'File a new flight plan, whatever.'

Sienna was packing when the bedroom door opened and Finn stood there.

She'd agonized over her decision to run away for a couple of hours after she'd gone out to the nearest chemist and bought a pregnancy test kit, and the test had proved positive. But it was the only thing that seemed to make sense to her.

She knew she couldn't bear the weight of Finn's disbelief in her, but to be pregnant at the same time made her feel even more deeply vulnerable, and trapped.

Of course, she would have to come to some arrangement with Finn but at least to be away from him might help her to set some of her own terms.

To see him standing in the doorway, so tall and commanding in jeans and a light grey sweater, caused her to shake like a leaf in a gale and grab one of the bedposts for support.

'Finn,' she breathed, 'what are you doing here?'

He closed the door and came over to the bed. 'What are *you* doing? What's wrong?' he said quietly but intensely.

She stared up at him. There were harsh lines scored beside his mouth, but something else in his eyes— concern? she wondered dazedly. But why?

'I—' she licked her lips '—I—'

But that blue gaze had roamed from her suitcase to the bedside table where the incriminating evidence of the pregnancy test, the packaging, still lay. He frowned and walked over to the table to pick the packet up and turn it over in his fingers.

He drew in an audible breath and his gaze flew back to hers. 'You're pregnant? When did you suspect it?'

She swallowed. 'When I lost my breakfast this morning, I stopped to think and count. It hadn't occurred to me,' she said anguishedly, 'before that but, of course, it should have.'

'So you were going to run away?' He came back to her and took her shoulders in his hands.

'Finn, there's no future for us that I can see,' she said bravely, although she was ashen now with blue smudges like bruises beneath her eyes. 'But I would never have hidden your child from you. I—I—*we* will have to make some arrangement, that's all.'

'All,' he marvelled.

'Well, what do you suggest?' she cried, goaded into exposing her frustration on top of her misery. 'You don't trust me—that's something I can't live with. But it's not only over James and Dakota that I find that lack of trust unbearable—you should have told me about Holly right from the start.'

His hands clenched on her shoulders until she winced. He immediately removed them and shoved them into his pockets.

'Look,' he said, 'apart from Declan, no one knew I had any reason to break up with Holly so I got left in the awful position of everyone assuming I was devastated after the accident. And in a way I was, I'd never wished that on anyone.' He stopped and sighed. 'I also had no wish to speak ill of the dead even though it was a betrayal that—' he pulled a hand out of his pocket and flipped it '—left me extremely cynical. So I decided to close the book and I did the same for Declan.'

'And you couldn't even open it for me?' she whispered.

He stared past her and his eyes were so bleak, she shivered. 'No,' he said at last, 'although maybe that was a mistake. But I was also protecting Declan.'

'You don't even like Declan,' she protested. 'How so, anyway? Holly got it wrong!'

'Holly didn't get it wrong.'

'But you told me—'

'Declan is my legitimate heir but not because he's my half-brother, he's my first cousin—he's my only cousin.'

Sienna gasped.

'His mother was having an affair with my father's brother, my uncle Bradley, who died in the same accident as my father and Laura. She was doing it right under my father's nose, in other words. But, while I may not have much time for Declan in some ways, that's not his fault.'

Sienna sat down on the bed; her legs didn't seem to want to support her.

'So you d-decided not to expose Declan?' she stammered.

Finn switched his gaze to her. 'Would you have? Not to mention all the dirty linen that went with it. Besides, it doesn't change one thing. He's my closest relative. Anyway,' he said harshly, 'I was sick to death of all the betrayals that had gone on, all the trauma—I just wanted to put it all behind me.'

Sienna grappled with the enormity of what Finn had been through, with the way he'd stuck by Declan despite their differences, but was it enough? she wondered. She'd bared her heart to him only to have it thrown back at her; he had, only by accident, been forced to confide in her and even then kept something back. Would that always be a sticking point for her? Could she love him with—talk about betrayal—her own feeling of betrayal planted in her heart?

'Would you have?' he asked again.

'Probably not,' she breathed. 'So—why have you told me this now, Finn?'

'Because this, this news, changes things,' he said.

Does it? she asked herself. How?

'It may for you. It doesn't for me, Finn.'

'Sienna—' he moved the suitcase and sat down beside her '—we can't only think of ourselves now.'

'I'm not. I'm thinking of bringing up a baby in a war zone.'

He picked up her hand and threaded his fingers through hers. 'Then let's declare peace.' He paused and fiddled with her wedding ring. 'You seemed to be really happy at Waterford.' She didn't see the particularly acute way he was watching her.

She shrugged. 'I loved Waterford.' Then she sniffed and looked around suddenly. 'I used to like Eastwood but now—' She broke off.

'What say we move to Waterford?'

Sienna stared at his lean brown fingers entwined with her own, but saw Waterford in her mind's eye, somehow breaking through the leaden, wet-cardboard mess that was her emotions. The gardens, the house, the golf course, the kids. She thought that it would probably raise no comment at all if she went back part-time to the Augathella Hospital physiotherapy unit for as long as she could…

She thought of where she would go otherwise. Her parents? She flinched. Endure a pregnancy on her own?

'So—are you suggesting we—sort of—start again?' she asked disjointedly.

'Yes.'

'Things could never be the same again, though,' she warned. 'Even if you do find Dakota and exonerate me.' Her voice was bitter. 'But I guess if you can close a book, so can I and I don't, honestly, know what else to do…' She looked at him suddenly. 'Why are you here? Why did you come back or didn't you ever go?'

'I went,' he said dryly. 'I turned back because I was worried about you. Some—instinct—got to me. I guess there's an invisible tie between us now.'

Sienna waited with bated breath for him to add— whether we like it or not.

He didn't. He pulled his hand free and put his arm around her shoulders. 'We'll get away from here as soon as possible. I'm not too fond of it myself.'

'Will you still try to track Dakota down?'

'No. This is a new book, Sienna, for both of us.'

CHAPTER ELEVEN

'SIENNA,' Mrs Walker admonished, 'you may not show it but you're four months pregnant. Why are you digging in the garden? It's not as if you don't have someone to do it for you! I really need eyes in the back of my head with you,' she added.

'I love digging in the garden.' Sienna rested her foot on the fork and her hands on the handle. 'Don't Chinese women work in the rice paddies right up until their babies are due?'

'I wouldn't know,' the cook said severely, 'but they should know better if they do. Anyway, Miss McLeod is due shortly.'

Sienna frowned. 'Shortly? I thought she was coming tomorrow.'

'She's not driving, she's hitched a lift with Declan, who is flying. He's just called in on the VHF and he's due soon.'

'Oh, no!' Sienna grimaced. 'How many people is he bringing with him?'

'I don't know. There was a lot of static on the line so I couldn't understand half of what he said, but the Green

House got a good clean out a couple of days ago and I've got plenty of food. I've sent a message to Finn, he's only out at the two-mile bore. Come inside now and get cleaned up.'

'Yes, Mum,' Sienna said meekly, but she patted Mrs Walker's shoulder and grinned at her. She left her gardening efforts with a tinge of regret, though.

Not that she minded Alice's frequent visits, but it was a magnificent winter's day with a clear, deep blue sky overhead, hot enough in the sun but extremely chilly overnight now, but that contrast was something she appreciated.

It was lovely to snuggle up in bed with an electric blanket or sit in front of a log fire.

In fact, as she showered she reflected on how Waterford had saved her from an abyss of misery.

Not that things were right between her and Finn, they never could be, although they'd become adept at hiding the true state of affairs between them.

But gathering up the strands of her earlier days on the station had kept her sane and even brought her a measure of peace. It had certainly brought her plenty to do on top of the half-days she spent at the hospital.

Walt, on learning that they would essentially be relocating to Waterford, had suggested that Eastwood would only need a skeleton staff and asked for six months' long leave.

Dave had moved on.

So it was Sienna who ran the household now, who was in charge of the gardens and a lot else besides. She also helped out in the school and had started a couple of schemes of her own. She'd formed a choir amongst, not only the station kids, but anyone who cared to join, and had been pleasantly surprised by some of the adult voices. She was even thinking of recording some of their songs.

She'd been banned from refereeing any mad forms of football—as Finn had put it—so she'd started, rather tongue in cheek, a bowls club one night a week. Again, it was not only the kids who participated and loved it.

So her life had become pleasant and fulfilling and her pregnancy had run smoothly after some weeks of morning sickness.

It also, while it might not show to others, showed to her now. Her breasts were fuller, her waist no longer so reed-slim.

One thing she found strange, however—her mind was not full of her coming baby. It was hard to visualize it; she had no urge to be decorating a nursery or gathering a layette. If it weren't for the evidence of her figure she could almost imagine she wasn't pregnant.

She did also sometimes stop and wonder what had made her do it—come back to Waterford with Finn. What had made her agree to this companionable, up to a point, life with him.

Of course it had been the sensible thing to do, but she hadn't been feeling very sensible at the time. She'd been heartbroken and bitter.

So had he been right about the invisible thread between them?

Not that she had that on her mind as she dressed in grey corduroy trousers and a lilac cashmere sweater as she heard the plane buzz the homestead.

All she had on her mind as she brushed her hair and slid her feet into grey suede flatties was how many people Declan would be inflicting on Waterford, and, by implication, Declan himself.

Was he still with Tara? she wondered.

It had proved to be a turbulent, on-off affair, but then Declan could have his own demons after Holly…

And she did sometimes think of the tortured relationship between Declan and Finn and how Holly Pearson had thought she could work it to her advantage.

But it wasn't Tara Finn drove to the homestead with Alice and Declan, it was Dakota.

Dakota, who had taken herself off to India after cancelling her wedding to James Haig, and who had managed to remain incommunicado apart from the odd call to their mother to assure her she was fine, she just needed to do her own thing for a while.

Sienna stopped as if shot as she stepped over the doorstep to greet the party, but Dakota ran up the stairs and flung her arms around Sienna.

It also shot through Sienna's mind as her sister hugged her joyfully to wonder if Dakota had the slightest idea of the mayhem she'd caused.

'Darling, it's so wonderful to see you and to see you looking wonderful! Not only that, I believe I'm to be an aunt.' Dakota released Sienna, patted her tummy gently and she turned to Finn standing on the top step with a bag in his hand.

'Oh, I knew you were so right for each other,' she said to him. 'I could just see it and it was seeing it in Sienna that made me understand James and I didn't *have* it, so you two saved me from making an awful mistake!'

Sienna was sitting by the fireside in her bedroom when the door to Finn's adjoining bedroom opened and he came in.

It was after ten o'clock and everyone had gone to bed, but she was still dressed. She had no lights on, only the firelight.

It had been a pleasant evening.

Dakota had revealed she'd gone to Eastwood after flying in from Mumbai, where Mrs Lawson had put her onto Alice, who'd just changed her plans. She would fly to Waterford with Declan so why didn't Dakota come with them?

Dakota had accepted the offer with pleasure.

'Are you all right?' Finn said quietly and added a log to the fire before he sat down opposite.

'Yes, no,' she said. 'How could we have been so right for each other and have it all end in—dust?'

'Your sister—'

But Sienna held up a hand.

'My sister is gorgeous, she can be thoughtless, she's always been a law unto herself. I've gone through feeling responsible for her as a kid, being exasperated by her as an adult then resenting her bitterly—' she heaved a sigh '—but in the end she's—my sister Dakota.'

'So she's not to blame for anything? Not even garbled messages capable of being misinterpreted before she walked away—and left everyone to pick up the pieces, incidentally?'

'No, Finn. It was your interpretation of those messages that was wrong. And, look, if you're going to tell me Dakota has exonerated me of what you suspected so it can all be…hunky-dory between us now, it's not going to work. Nor do I want to go through it all again. I've got myself together and I need to keep myself together.'

She laid her head back wearily.

He watched the reflected firelight flicker on the pallor of her face.

'Just tell me one thing, Sienna. What happened on our wedding night?'

Her lashes fluttered. 'If you really want to know, Finn, I was battling, not a cupboard full of demons, just one. I was battling Holly.'

His shock was palpable. 'You didn't even know Holly!'

'No, I didn't. But, at the time, I didn't know either what your memories were, whether you could ever love me the way you'd loved her. I tried to stop myself thinking about it. I told myself she was gone, but she somehow got to me that night—or the fear of how I would cope if I didn't measure up to her did. You see, I was so very much in love with you.'

He stared at her transfixed.

'Dakota obviously saw it before I had—well—' she gestured '—before I'd actually admitted the true extent of it to myself. It just, I don't know,' she said barely audibly, 'boiled up in me that night and I knew it would hurt me terribly if I didn't replace Holly in your heart.'

'So you didn't marry me because you couldn't have James?'

'Do you know,' she said slowly, 'I fooled myself about James.' Her shoulders lifted. 'I think I'd decided it was time—I *was* twenty-four—I fell in love otherwise I could be a bit of a freak. But the hurt associated with that was actually far more to do with Dakota than James. Silly, probably—' she linked her fingers '—not to see it for so long but—' she raised her eyes to his '—you're wrong if you think I haven't agonized over my sister.'

'And you didn't decide to marry me as a way to ensure your own children and a location you seemed to love?' he said after a long pause, and he looked around.

Sienna blinked. 'Of course not—is that what you thought?'

'I wondered. I wondered all sorts of things, Sienna, and do you know why?'

She shook her head.

'Because I didn't realize just how much of a cynic I'd become. It never occurred to me that to see you in James Haig's arms would drive me crazy with jealousy, and land me right back in the kind of turmoil I went through with Holly, or so I thought.'

'*Jealousy?*' she repeated.

'Yes.' He looked grim. 'But even before that, it never occurred to me that seeing you so distraught on our wedding night would affect me so much. That's when I started looking for—skeletons. That's when it came back to me, all Holly's machinations, and wouldn't let me go.' He pushed his hand through his hair savagely.

She made a strange little sound.

'Until I realized belatedly that what Holly had dented was my pride, not my heart.' He looked into the fire for a moment, then into her eyes. 'I don't only want you in my arms and in my bed, Sienna. I want to know I'm the only one in your heart because that's what had happened to me. I fell in *love* with you whereas I fell in lust with Holly. The differences are breathtaking.'

'Tell me,' she said huskily.

He looked into the fire for a long moment. 'There's no pride involved with you, but I won't ever be the same again if I lose you.'

'But right up until a few minutes ago you were still querying my motives,' she said shakily. 'Almost as if it was the same old story. You couldn't believe that having put myself right in the firing line, bound myself to you in the closest way but not knowing if you could ever love me back in the same way, made me feel…absolutely terrible.'

He turned back slowly. 'Are you sure?'

'More sure of that than anything else.' Tears glittered in her eyes. 'Then to have James flung at me, and Dakota, and the fact that you couldn't tell me the truth about Holly—' She stopped and blinked rapidly.

'Killed it all for you, Sienna?'

'I—I don't know,' she whispered. 'What made you tell me this tonight if it wasn't Dakota?'

'I'm—' he shoved his hands in his pockets '—I'm unbearably lonely. I'm constantly reminded of all the things I took for granted—not for granted, but all the gifts you bestowed on me that I didn't fully appreciate until they were gone. But it was Dakota in a way—and something else.'

'How was it Dakota?' she breathed.

'She obviously saw what I was too blind to see at the time. Too mindful that I needed to be in control of myself, which certainly wasn't consistent with handing you my heart. Not to know,' he said with dreadful self-directed irony, 'it was going to lose me yours.'

Sienna stared up at him with her lips parted as she saw the pain in his eyes.

'Gifts?' she said cautiously.

He shrugged. 'The perfume of your skin I can never forget. The way you made love to me as if,' he said with an effort, 'you're a dancing flame only I can bring to light. The way I'm bored and miserable without you. And I mean without, not only your presence, but when you shut yourself off from me as you have. The light, for that matter, you bring to so many lives.

'And,' he went on, 'I can never forget that instinct that told me I was deserting you in your hour of need after I'd flown out for Perth.' He closed his eyes. 'I may not have been a great help at the time, a lot of it was all new to me, but you drew me back—you always will, Sienna. Wherever you go, whatever you do, will affect me. I'm sorry.'

'Finn—' She couldn't go on.

'But what really worries me is—and I knew I couldn't let it go any longer even if you wanted me to— I can't see any joy in you about the baby. I know, I know—' he gestured '—the circumstances may not be ideal but—' He stopped.

'Oh, Finn—' she stumbled up suddenly, her eyes urgent, her mouth working '—how did you know?

There's nothing. There's this void, as if it isn't happening to me. Something seems to tell me I can only be happy and peaceful if I don't think about the baby.'

'Could,' he said huskily, 'that be to do with the void the baby's father created in your life because he was such a bloody fool?'

'*Yes*—I mean—'

'I was, Sienna.' He took her hands in his. 'But I'd give anything to be able to make amends. Anything.'

She stared up into his eyes and couldn't, at last, doubt him. Not only from the torture she saw in his eyes, but because he'd read her so accurately. He'd seen below the calm, collected face she'd presented to the world, he'd divined *her* inner torture, and only someone who, not only knew her almost better than she did, but also cared deeply about her could have done that.

'Oh, Finn…' her voice trembled '…hold me, please. I've missed you so much too.'

He cupped her face first as if still unsure he could believe her, as if he was still waiting for some blow that was more than he could bear.

'Please,' she repeated.

He swept her into his arms.

'These have changed,' he said slightly unsteadily.

They were in the same bed where they'd first made love, his bed, and there was ample evidence of this lovemaking. The sheets and covers were rumpled and thrust aside and Sienna was in glorious disarray, with her hair spread over the pillow, her limbs gilded by the firelight, her eyes dark and dreamy, her mouth ripe.

'Yes,' she agreed as he touched her breasts, then she looked into his eyes. 'You remember them exactly?'

'I remember them perfectly. And this has changed.' He put his hands on her waist. 'I used to be able to almost span it. But these haven't changed.' He cupped her hips, then leant his head on his elbow and looked down at her ruefully. 'Do you know when I first pictured you swinging your naked hips at me?'

Her lips parted. 'No…'

'When you walked away from me at Angelo's in a high dudgeon.' He circled her lips with his fingertips and smiled reflectively. 'It had a very powerful effect on me.'

Sienna took a breath then her lips trembled into a smile. 'If only I'd known.'

'You'd have inflicted even more damage on my self-control?' he hazarded.

'No.' She shook her head. 'I wouldn't have been so convinced only I was subject to tingly moments between us.'

He gathered her closer and said into her hair, 'I'm sorry. But I wasn't aware—tingly?' He lifted his head and looked into her eyes.

'Uh-huh,' she agreed. 'That was the first of many, that night, but it was a while before I stopped putting them down to the inevitable effect you had on most women, probably.'

He grimaced. 'You hid it all well.' He stroked her shoulder. 'I have to confess that riled me.' He pulled her even closer, close and urgent. 'I should have known it was a precursor to not being able to live without you,' he added, with his voice roughened by emotion.

'Finn.' She clasped his head in her hands, then stopped and her eyes widened, her lips parted.

'What?' he breathed.

'It moved.' She removed her hands and clasped them over her belly.

He sat up with anxiety etched in his eyes. 'Is something wrong?'

'No.' She sat up herself with a growing look of wonder in her eyes. 'No, it's supposed to—oh! There it is again. It's a bit like a butterfly—oh, Finn, it's real at last.'

'You don't suppose it's objecting to us—to us—'

She turned her shining gaze to him. 'I think it's giving us a seal of approval, that's what I think, and it's made me feel just—wonderful.'

'All the same, I shall desist until I get your doctor's approval.'

Sienna looked at him with so much tenderness he took an unexpected breath.

'I see,' she said gravely, however.

'See what?' he queried

'Well, your aunt worries about me like a mother hen. Mrs Walker, ditto, she definitely does not approve of the rice-paddy approach for pregnant women!'

'What the hell is that?' he asked with a comic look of apprehension.

Sienna explained.

'No wonder!' he responded. 'Neither do I.'

'So you've added yourself to a bit of a list of worriers, Finn,' she told him.

'Ah. As a matter of fact—' he pulled her into his arms and lay back with her and drew up the covers

'—I've been watching you like a hawk when I've been here and I may have instigated that list for when I haven't.'

'May have?'

'Yes. Well, I'm sure Alice and Mrs Walker would have done so anyway, but actually there's a whole network of watchers, all of Waterford. Just in case you're tempted to ride—anything, let alone a horse that's too big for you or anything else dicey.'

Sienna attempted to sit up with a protest on her lips, but she subsided and started to laugh. 'I love you,' she said instead. 'I really love you, Finn.'

A powerful tremor rocked him. 'I love you, Sienna.' He looked deep into her eyes, then kissed her deeply.

Seven months later Sophie McLeod participated in her christening with what could only be described as aplomb.

At two months old, she had blue eyes and a fluffy down of fair hair. Her cheeks were round, there was a dimple in her chin, she had a rosebud mouth and a contented nature—when she wasn't hungry. When she was, there was a determination about her that reminded her mother rather particularly of her father.

She had also taken Waterford by storm, and not only Waterford. She received an amazing number of visitors. Her great-aunt was often in residence, her maternal grandparents showed a similar tendency. People from all over the district and further afield popped in until Mrs Walker, who was actually a great fan herself, was heard to remark nevertheless that you'd think no one had ever seen a baby before.

The station kids were rapt. They even ran raffles—when she'd smile for the first time was the current one.

'Do you ever get the feeling we've been trumped, gazumped, we're kind of non-events these days, Mrs McLeod?' Finn said to Sienna once. 'No one asks me how I am any more. I could be tottering to my grave for all they care! It's always—how's the baby? How the hell does one tiny little person who hasn't said a word yet, although there's no doubt she has a voice, achieve that?'

Sienna laughed and admitted she'd wondered the same thing. 'I think she just has a presence,' she said. 'Or maybe they're very happy for us and she's the positive proof of it so she gets all the kudos?'

Finn looked down at Sophie lying on a rug in the dappled sunshine, kicking her legs and gurgling. 'She does have a presence.' His face softened. 'She's gorgeous, aren't you, pumpkin?' He put one finger into Sophie's hand and her tiny starfish fingers closed around it tightly.

'You're not going to call her that for the rest of her life, are you?' Sienna queried.

'Possibly. What's wrong with it?' He looked a little put out. 'I like it, and it might be a good idea to have my own private name for her since I frequently have to battle my way through hordes of her admirers.'

Sienna leant over the baby and kissed him swiftly. 'Finn, I never dreamt you could be so—like this over a baby. Maybe as she grew up a bit but—' She shook her head.

'Ah, but I'm very selective,' he teased. 'If I didn't happen to be deeply, madly in love with this baby's mother, I don't suppose I'd feel the same. Makes all the difference in the world.'

'You say the nicest things sometimes.'

'I mean them. All set for the christening?'

Sienna drew a deep breath. 'I think so, but talk about hordes!' She gestured and looked a little nervous.

'We'll cope,' he reassured her.

It was a great success, the christening.

The same minister who had married Finn and Sienna performed the ceremony on a cloudless, beautiful day. Sophie wore a gorgeous lace gown and didn't object to having her head bathed.

A feast had been set out in the garden on long tables covered with pink cloths and the christening cake was a masterpiece of intricate icing, pink rosebuds on white trellis. Champagne flowed.

Every station kid had been scrubbed, combed within an inch of their lives, and wore their best clothes.

It was during the photo session that Finn took Sienna's hand.

Sophie had been passed to her grandparents, her great-aunt and was now with her godparents, Declan and Dakota.

Sienna watched, with a lump in her throat as they both looked down at the baby in Dakota's arms, with unmistakable pride.

Dakota had a new beau, a quiet man but one who seemed to generate a new maturity in her sister.

Declan hadn't separated from Tara; he'd married her some months ago. From a turbulent on-off relationship, their marriage had worked well and had steadied Declan considerably, and even Alice had overcome her aversion to Tara. And as they watched Declan beckoned to Tara to join him and Dakota.

That was when Finn said, a little unsteadily and only audibly to Sienna, 'I can't thank you enough.'

Sienna glanced at him, standing by her side so tall and attractive in a beautiful grey suit but staring straight ahead. 'What for?' she murmured. 'We—'

'No,' he broke in, '*you* rescued my life from a smoking ruin, Sienna.' His fingers gripped hers almost unbearably tightly for a moment.

'Oh, Finn,' she whispered, 'no. We both went through the mill, but it's made us stronger and better.'

He looked down at her at last. She wore a slim jade silk dress and her hair was loose, as he liked it best. Motherhood had brought a luminescence to her that he found breathtaking.

'I have a slight difficulty,' he confessed.

Sienna looked concerned. 'But it's going so well!'

'Am I allowed to kiss the mother of the baby? Otherwise I'll be seriously indisposed.'

Sienna let out a breath of relief. 'Oh, I think so.'

He put his arms around her, but in the moment before he suited action to words he said, with his heart in his eyes, 'I will never be able to thank you enough, my darling Sienna, never.'

When they drew apart her heart was beating wildly with love, joy and fulfilment—and everyone applauded delightedly.

I ♥ HARLEQUIN Presents

BROUGHT TO YOU BY FANS OF
HARLEQUIN PRESENTS.

We are its editors and authors
and biggest fans—and we'd
love to hear from YOU!

Subscribe today to our online blog at
www.iheartpresents.com

REQUEST YOUR FREE BOOKS!

2 FREE NOVELS
PLUS 2
FREE GIFTS!

YES! Please send me 2 FREE Harlequin Presents® novels and my 2 FREE gifts (gifts are worth about $10). After receiving them, if I don't wish to receive any more books, I can return the shipping statement marked "cancel". If I don't cancel, I will receive 6 brand-new novels every month and be billed just $4.05 per book in the U.S. or $4.74 per book in Canada, plus 25¢ shipping and handling per book and applicable taxes, if any*. That's a savings of close to 15% off the cover price! I understand that accepting the 2 free books and gifts places me under no obligation to buy anything. I can always return a shipment and cancel at any time. Even if I never buy another book, the two free books and gifts are mine to keep forever. 106 HDN ERRW 306 HDN ERRL

Name _____ (PLEASE PRINT)

Address _____ Apt. #

City _____ State/Prov. _____ Zip/Postal Code

Signature (if under 18, a parent or guardian must sign)

Mail to the **Harlequin Reader Service:**
IN U.S.A.: P.O. Box 1867, Buffalo, NY 14240-1867
IN CANADA: P.O. Box 609, Fort Erie, Ontario L2A 5X3

Not valid to current subscribers of Harlequin Presents books.

Want to try two free books from another line?
Call 1-800-873-8635 or visit www.morefreebooks.com.

* Terms and prices subject to change without notice. N.Y. residents add applicable sales tax. Canadian residents will be charged applicable provincial taxes and GST. Offer not valid in Quebec. This offer is limited to one order per household. All orders subject to approval. Credit or debit balances in a customer's account(s) may be offset by any other outstanding balance owed by or to the customer. Please allow 4 to 6 weeks for delivery. Offer available while quantities last.

Your Privacy: Harlequin Books is committed to protecting your privacy. Our Privacy Policy is available online at www.eHarlequin.com or upon request from the Reader Service. From time to time we make our lists of customers available to reputable third parties who may have a product or service of interest to you. If you would prefer we not share your name and address, please check here. ☐

HP08R

MEDITERRANEAN DOCTORS

Demanding, devoted and
drop-dead gorgeous—
These Latin doctors will
make your heart race!

Smolderingly sexy Mediterranean doctors

Saving lives by day...red-hot lovers by night

**Read these four Mediterranean Doctors stories
in this new collection by your favorite authors,
available in Presents EXTRA October 2008:**

THE SICILIAN DOCTOR'S MISTRESS
by SARAH MORGAN

THE ITALIAN COUNT'S BABY
by AMY ANDREWS

SPANISH DOCTOR, PREGNANT NURSE
by CAROL MARINELLI

THE SPANISH DOCTOR'S LOVE-CHILD
by KATE HARDY

www.eHarlequin.com

HPE1008

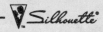

**FROM *NEW YORK TIMES*
BESTSELLING AUTHOR**

LINDA LAEL MILLER

A STONE CREEK CHRISTMAS

Veterinarian Olivia O'Ballivan finds the animals
in Stone Creek playing Cupid between her and
Tanner Quinn. Even Tanner's daughter, Sophie,
is eager to play matchmaker. With everyone
conspiring against them and the holiday season
fast approaching, Tanner and Olivia may just get
everything they want for Christmas after all!

*Available December 2008
wherever books are sold.*